Fading Away

Alfie Noble

Contents

Prologue

He saw her, he came to know her, he loved her. But she never crossed the first step to fall in love with him. She looked at him but never saw him. Not really. he was just the eldest son of the family which had been her second home in a foreign land, nothing more. But he wanted to be a lot more, the most. So, like a sculptor he began to shape her future, one that would include him, revolve around him. But a sculptor owns their art and he never owned her, specially someone whose passion was their first priority and marriage not even their last. Even if he can shape it, would it really be a victory because the voices in her head, the shadow looming over her soul and the darkness altogether may not let her live if not in her way. And what would her best friend do when he would see the pieces he had help her put together and bind carefully, fall apart? Who had been with her through every up and down ,had helped her cross it. Standing by her, helping her walk through it was the goal but it might come at the cost of self destruction for her preservation.

Chapter 1:crazy,silly best friend

I ANA'S POV:

Ring... Ring...

My cell kept ringing and after 3 rings I finally receive it.

"It's 1 A.M as of now,"I say grumpily,letting the caller at the opposite end know that I am not pleased.

"I missed you,"came the voice from the other end, small.

"At one in the morning!!"My voice incredulous.It's hard to restrain it now.

"Skyler broke up with me,"Now came the real reason,"OVER TEXT!!"

I couldn't help rolling my eyes and sat up properly kind of knowing this is gonna be long..I had to bite my tongue to keep myself from saying-Told you so or what are you sad about?That she broke up with you before you could with her.

Rather I just said a small,"Oh!"Like I am sad at this revealation.

I fixed a pillow behind my head and pulled the comforter to my neck waiting for him to start being dramatic.

"I did so much for her.I thought-I thought we were so happy but look at her she broke up with me over text.She didn't even meet me."

And what did I do?i just hummed well because that's what you do when it's about Ebenezer or Zer,as I say it.His phone battery last longer than his relationships.He would be like,I want a true relationship but I have never seen one of his last very long.

The rest of the night passesthrough his whining and complaining while I hum along untill we finally meet at the library at a 3;30.I had told him a thousand times to get rest because otherwise he would look like a literal zombie but he said and I quote,"He was in too much pain to bear alone!!"

The rest of the library passes with sudden exclamation here and there "but how could she break up with me?I am so handsome." And sitting with slouched shoulders as if just fed up with life in deep thought accompanied by occasional long,sad sighs.

Now don't blame me that I couldn't hide the laugh that escaped me.he was being extra ridiculous and I can bet that the only reason he is grumpy because he got dumped.

First forward to first lecture,he is sitting with a sunglass indoors because his he wants sleep and also he does look like a zombie.

He has dozed off in the seat right beside mine,slouching to one side and the professor voice makes him wake up a with a startle,trying to figure out what happened before he finally gets it.

Of course it doesn't go unnoticed by professor who remarks,"A advice for a couple of extra skilled students.Go home and sleep rather then wasting your time and parents money here."

I hear Zer grumble beside.

Later when we are in the cafeteria with his head hanging behind the chair and sitting at an angle with the table"I have decide,"He says with determination and I mumble to myself,here ' comes the part', of course out of his hearing,"I won't waste any more time on her.I have moved on.She didn't deserve e anyway."

"You hardly wasted any on her actually.It's been what...11 hours and.....20 minutes give or take."I say after a look at my clock."That's a new record though."

"I am trying to be serious Iana,"He rebukes.

"Oh!I know.it's just that your sleep sessions last longer than this."I give him the sweetest smile I can measure and he keeps on his grumpy face,hoodie on and headset covered ears.

That's how Zer is.Right now he is just grumpy but what he always is-is my best friend.

He is crazy,silly,funny a total dummy but when you need him he will be your strength and I am saying that from experience.

"Get someone else to listen to your whining because I have to leave for the book shop now."

"You are gonna leave me in a time like this?Really Iana?"

I couldn't help rolling my eyes.

****

I am at the bookshop.It's almost time to close now and I am just finishing the last bits of work.

After I finally closing I return to dorm, getting ready to go to bed.

This is what my days looks like minus the whiny Zer..Well,a good one anyway.It has been consisting of those recently. The fog is maybe starting to clear off.

Vote and comment.I know it's boring but it will get better.

Chapter 2:A second family

In this chapter Iana's relationship with Ehan's family is explained,more or less.I know it is pretty long and boring but it was important.

IANA'S POV:

Like always these guys are late.Almost ten minutes have passed and still there is no sign of them and sitting alone in this café makes me feel like a artifact in a museum on which every eye is situated,speculating with everything in them.After another five minutes Ayesha and Humaira and enter the café and like always are prepared with their excuses.

"has kiun rahi ho.Tumhe pata hai ready hone mein kitna bakt lagta hein."humaira said.(why are you laughing?Do you know how much time it takes someone to get ready?)

"Bilkul nahi.Mein to ready na hokar hi ay gain hoon."I reply while laughing.My voice dripping with sarcasm when humaira punches my arm playfully.(Not at all.As if I came here without getting ready.)

"Hanan api aj bhi nahi ayi,"I ask though I know the answer well enough.(Hanan api didn't come today as well.)

"Are woh aur unke kam!!"Humaira sighs.(She and her work!!)

"Hmm.Hanan api bohat hard working hei.Allah kare ki hum bhi future me itne hard working aur passionate bane,"I say and it is absolutely true.I admire hanan api for her determination and skills.She is absolutely amazing.She,Ibrahim bhaijan and Ehan bhaijan take care of the company,the three eldest heirs.(Hmm.Hanan api is very hardworking and passionate,May Allah help me become this much hardworking and passionate in future.)

"Are Iana agar isse jyada kam karne lagi to robot ban jaogi,"Ayesha says.(Hey,Iana if you work any more then you will turn into a robot.)

"Abhi nahi hei kya,"Humaira says and they both burst out laughing.(Isn't she one now!)

"come on.guys,"I can't help saying annoyed at these two.

Our whole afternoon passes like this-eating,laughing and catching up.

when we are about to leave Ayesha says,"Iana,aj tum hamare sath ghar aa rahi ho aur Hanan se bhi mil lena.Bari Ammi bhi yumhare bare mein puch rahi thi."(Iana.you are coming home with us and you can meet Hanan there as well.Evan Bari Ammi was asking about you.)

"But"I hardly start when Humaira interrupts me with,"And no excuses."

A small smile escapes me and I say,"Thik hei,chalo."syed Mansion somehow feels like home and everyone absolutely adores me there. (Okay,let's go.)

After reaching syed mansion we head straight to the lounge where we spot everyone having snacks and just chilling.Just after seeing me Malak aunty engulfs me in a hug and after that she asks me."Bete,kasi ho.Kitne din bad aa rahi ho aur call to tum karti nahi"(Bete,how are you.You are coming after so many days and you don't call anyway.)

I guilty look crosses my face because she is absolutely right.I hardly if ever call people.it is most of the time malak aunty who calls me.Not the other way around.

"Actually aunty recently bohat busy thy".(Actually aunty,I was recently very busy)

"to phir hamare liye samai nahi nikalogi kaye."(Then won't you find some time for us.)

"maf kar dein,please"(Forgive me,please)

"bete parhai ke bahar bhi ek duniya hei.Use enjoy karo,thik kei?"(Bete,there is a world outside studies as well.Learn to enjoy it,okay?)

"jee aunty."(Okay,aunty.)

"are vabi sari bat khare hokar hi karengi kayen.Iana ko bethne dein."Hanifa aunty inbterjects.(vabi,will you ask about everything while standing.Let Iana sit down."

"ha Iana aao betho."Aamira aunty adds.(Yes,Iana, come sit down.)

"ha par,Pehle tumhare Dadaji se mil lo."Malak aunty says.(yes but meet your grandpa first)

Malak aunty had once told me that he see his his daughter in me.her name was Aabroo.She committed suicide at a very young age.Once even Dadaji had said kind of dazed,"Bilkul meri Aabroo ki tara," and I try to live by that role as much as I can.

Following aunty's advice I go to the room and softly knock on the door.After hearing a come in I enter the room.Smilling at me,he says,"kechi ho,mere bachi."(How are you my child?)

"jee,dadagi thik hoon.Aap kese hain.Apni dabai to bakt par le rehe hain na."(Grandpa,I am fine.How are you?You are taking your medicines on time,right?"

"ha bilkul.Ab ati kiun nahi hoon.Kisi baat se naraz hoo."(Yes.Why don't you come here anymore.Are you angry about something?)

"Bilkul nahi.Bas schedule thora hectic hai."(Not at all.it is just that my schedule is a bit hectic.)

"beta,jan hain to jahan hai.Yeh baat humesha yad rakhna."(Beta,h ealth is wealth.Always remember this.)

"jee."(Yes.)

After talking with dadaji a bit more I return to the lounge.Th e youngstars have replaced their their elder and peace is definitely something foreign to them.They are really loud and unlike most other loud I like this loud but instead of joining their conversation I like to listen to them.Rather than participating in it I am having fun just seeing them have fun and moreover.But that doesn't mean that I always just sit back with them I participate most times.

Arhan says,"And like always Iana ia working."

"sor...."I start when Haya interjects"AND DON'T SAY SORRY."

Of course everyone laughs while my cheeks become hot.They always tease me with my habit of saying sorry.

"Actually,the project is really coming together so these days are a bit hectic."I explain the reason.

"Aur apke konse din hectic nahi hotein."(And which day is not hectic for you.)Irfan teases me when Aamira aunty says,"Not everyone is lazy like whose life is literally eat,sleep and repeat." glaring at him.She was just passing by and heard our conversation.

"kya ammi!"Irfan whines and laughter is again renewed but the reason is different.I turn my attention to the laptop again so that I can save the changes and finally put it away.

After dinner we all are in the garden,meaning all the cousin but everybody else has gone to sleep.It is pretty late,almost 12:30 a.m. Past my bedtime but they wouldn't let me go and so I joined.Now Ibrahim bhaijan and Hanan is also with us.

We all are absolutely engrossed when a car enters the driveway.

"YE TO EHAN BHAIJAN KI CAR HE.WOH AYE HEI KYA?'Arhan whisper yells.

"PAR UNHONE TO INFORM BHI NAHI KIYA,"It's humaira's turn now.

"Apne ghar ane ki liye inform karna parega kya or sab bethe kiun ho.Clean kar ye sad jaldi.Bhaijan ko ase gatherings or itne ratko bilkul bhi pasand nahi ayaga,"It's Hanan.the always calm and collected Ha nan.(Now,does he have to inform to come to his own house and why are you all still sitting.clean all this fast.Bhaijan doesn't like these kind of gatherings and not this late at night.)

She and Ibrahim bhaijan approaches Ehan bhaijan and we all clean the space because it was a mess with all the snacks and everything.But I am absolutely clueless about what is going on.

The three of them enter in the house and after one hell of a cleaning session we all enter as well.

I am a bit hesitant and I stop abruptly at the door.After all this seems like a family thing and moreover I have never met Ehan bhaijan.I have heard of him multiple times.It always seemed more or less he controls what happens here.So,it seems like invading.

"Iana,why are you standing here.Let's go in."Arhan asks me.

"It seems like invading.Don't you think it would be better if I wait here."

"Majak na kiya karo," and with that he drags me in the house with him.(Don't joke around!)

When we enter we see that Ehan bhaijan,(I don't know what else to call him and I call Ibrahim bhaijan that so.....) has already left and entered his room.

"Sabko uthana chaiye tha na?"Humaira asks.(We should have waked everyone uo,right?)

"Bhaijan ne mana kya hae.Unhone kaha ki kal subha sabse mil lenge."Haya answers.(Bhaijan,forbade us,he said that he would meet everybody tomorrow morning.)

"Par phir bhi sab datange.After all ghar ka favourite do sal bad aya hai."And everyone sighs at this.(Even then everybody would scold us.AFter all everyone's favourite has returned after 2 years.)

After a few more momments of chit-chatting everyone returns to their room and so do I.

Dadaji-grandpa

bhaijan-brother

api-siste

bari ammi-aunt

bete/bache-child,dear,used as an endearment

Please vote and comment.I will be really grateful if you do.

Untill next time,

Astral

Chapter 3:Awkward ride

ANA'S POV:

I just woke up a while ago,Right now I am sitting in the balcony,It,s still dark outside after all it's just 3.30 a.m.It is peaceful.To most people night is deceiving.It is deceitful.it is when the monsters come out.But to me it is peaceful.There is no hustle like the day. Night brings out our true form.Whatever we truly are and if we are monsters night won't shy away from brining that out as well.

Right that moment Zer calls me.He knows that I am awake.I It's been almost 2 years since I came to the USA and I met him in the very beginning.Both of us were sophomore year students.Our friendship started almost instantly.we first met in the library and within a short time,we became best friends.From then he has always been there for me.I talk with him for some time and then we both study while being on a group call.

At the breakfast table the next morning there is absolutely pin drop silence which is out of place because breakfast here is hardly quite.After everyone is done eating Ehan bhaijan clears his throat to get attention I guess and everyone's eyes trail to him.

"Tum sab yeha parhai bhi karte ho ye pura bakt phalto kamome barbad karte ho.Abhi bhi bakt hai,sudhar jao barna sab failures hi reh jaoge."(Do you all study at all here or waste all the time?You all still have a chance.Mend you ways otherwise you will stay as failures.)T hat was very rude considering that he wasn't here for 2 years.

"Irfan tumne apne last Anatomy exam me fail kya hai and Ayesha agar asa hi chalta raha to phir tumhae grade aur bhi drop hoga.Kar kya rahe ho tum sab.Mei yaha nahi hu iska matlab ye nahi hai ki mughe kuch bhi pata nahi he."(Irfan you failed your last anatomy exeam and SAyesha if this keeps going on then your grade will drop even more.What the hell are you all doing?)

Well,I take what I said back but still....

"Iana,you shouldn't have been exposed to it and forgive me for my misconduct but"a sharp look at others,"some people needed it."

He still has manners but he is way too strict.

the day passes in a breeze and afternoon arrives much sooner then I thought.I have to leave now as I have classes tomorrow.All the elders are in the lounge around this time.Seeing me,Malak aunty initiates the conversation,"Abhi ja rehi ho."(leaving now?)

"Ji aunty.kal class hain."(yes aunty.I have classes tomorrow.)

"abse phir weekends per aogi na."(You will come on the weekends,right?)

"koshish karungi."(I will try.)

"Koshish nahi results chaiye."(Trying is not enough.we want results.)

"thik hain"I say meekly because she won't let me leave otherwise. She is such a sweetheart.(okay)

"Kiske sath ja rehi ho.Ehan bhi abhi jaa raha hain.Tum uske sath chali jao."(whom are you going with?Ehan is also leaving.go with him)

"Aunty koi zaarurat nahi hai.Aiden ae hi raha hain."(Aunty,no need.Aiden is coming)

"are,use kiun taklif dena."Saying this she calls her son and tells him to drop me.(Why bother him?)

I realy wanted to avoid this.I am awkward beyond description with new people but yet here I am in his car in the back seat while his driver is driving.

"Please don't smoke.It's killing you."I can't help saying.I dont't know why I keep doing these things......

EHAN'S POV:

"Please don't smoke.It's killing you."She said.Not a order,neither a reprove nor laced with disdain but a plea.Her eyes are lowered while her hands fidget with each other.She seems nervous.She seems as if she didn't wanna say it but couldn't help herself.In any other case I would have probably silenced them with a glare and went on smoking as if they didn't even say anything.Actually anyone wouldn't even dare to say that to me.But she did and I couldn't turn her down.There was something in her voice as if it carried across the care it held.But the cause is not the question anymore because irrespective of what it was,I did throw away the cigarette for which she thanked me.We bit later we reached her dorm.

This girl,who is so dear to my family does have a way with things .You know when someone tries to order you around or forbid you from something you do it just to spite them but pleas are harder to deny.Moreover such a small request could very well be answered especially when presented in so delicate a way.

---

please vote and comment.

Chapter 4:Different opinions

ZER'S POV:

This girl is gonna be the death of me.I was supposed to pick her after she calls me but neither did she call me nor is she picking up my call.Should I call the police?Should I go there mys.................an d,there she is.

Before she even reaches me she says,"Sorry" with a face that even kids can't compete with.

"Yeah,right.A few more minutes and Police would have been the one greeting you and where is your phone?"I asked her.

She proceeded to take her phone out from her backpack which she has put on silent followed by a sorry with a guilty look which made it mandatory for me to facepalm which I did......mentally.This girl is never gonna mend her ways.

After a mild scolding session we went to the cafeteria to grab so mething.Iana is like rain,beautiful beyond description with altruism reining her very heart and always leaving a mark behind but the divinity offering that beauty sheds tears of pain which not many can see.It is condensed to the level that it can't take it anymore and it let's go.We appreciate the beauty but the pain hidden underneath escapes most.

Though she tries to alleviate everyone's pain,it hardly ever spares her.Pain might turn you into something broken and beautiful but that pain is only broken never beautiful.Her mental health issues started with her family.It's shocking what small things can add up to and that is exactly what happened to her.

She has issues with her family which might not seem much but added up like trees to form a forest which trapped her inside it.Forests are only beautiful when they offer you a leave from the cage you were previously behind,city life, not when they refuse to let you leave becoming a cage themselves.

Bi=ut I will be there for her,always.That's what friends are for,right?

IANA'S POV:

Soon we reach the designated place.I leave with a goodbye and see you soon.

After entering syed mansion and a lot of fun more like nuisance I enter my room almost at around 11 to sleep.Just when I am done making my bed I receive a call from my sister.

"Assalwalaikun apu,"I say.

"Walaikum assalam,ki korteso,"She asks me.(Walaikum as-salam,what are you doin?)

"ghumate jabo,just bed thik kortesilam,tumi?"(I am just about to sleep.What are you doing.)

"Ghamtesi.Prochur gorom."(Sweating.It is dangerously hot.)

:Ahare,bechara,"I say with a chuckle.(Poor baby)

"Ekhon hashtesen,thakle bujhten."(Now you are laughing.Only if you were here.)

"I very sincerely apologize,"i say with a funny seriousness.

Conversations like this go on for a bit longer before we finally hang up.My relationship with my siter is a long history but I am grateful that it is improving now.

It,s 3:30 and I am reading The Nightangle that Zer and I had choose.We always decide on a book an then read it and after finishing it choose another one.I reach for the water bottle and notice that it is empty.

Panir o akhoni shesh hoya lagto!(IT'S BANGLA)-I groan menta lly.(Even the water had to finish now!)

Now I have to go downstairs to get water,Whatever..

EHAN'S POV:

I just reached home.These few years I couldn't come home at all because I had just taken over the business I was too busy taking care of different branches it.Fixing the cracks.I was out of country most of the time.But now I am much more free when compared to earlier days.

When I am entering through the lounge I hear some noise from the kitchen.There is no way it is a thief because there are so many gaurds outside but still it is better to be safe than sorry.

Entering the kitchen,I see a girl getting a water bottle out from the refrigerator.This is not Ayesha,Haya or Hanan because they don't wear hijab and a scarf is wrapped around her head in a loose but secure hijab.

That's when she turns around to leave.Looks like Iana kept mom,s promise.(His mom had pressed her to visit on the weekends).She didn't expect to find someone here and seeing me all on a sudden definitely started her and consequently she dropped the opened bottle spilling water everywhere.

I was the one who scared her yet she says,"Ya Allah,I am so sorry." with a look much more guilty.

"I will just call a maid."

"No need.I will clean it."She says.

I look at her with a questioning gaze.

"It's almost 4 in the morning.It will be inhuman to wake them to fix a mess which I created.Morover,why bother someone else for something you can do?"She says and proceeds to clean it.Why would she wanna do it when someone else can do it for her.

"They are getting paid for it,"I say.

"But that doesn't mean they have to answer our every whim,"she says.

"It does actually,"When I say this she just looks at me shocked.

"There is something called compassion and if I were in that position I wouldn't wanna be treated like that.Allah placed us in comfortable situations but that doesn't mean we have to misuse it."

Now,I squat right in front of her and say,"You don't have to compassionate for this whole world and They are here to serve you."

"I don't have to be but I want to be and they are here to make our life easier and we should do the same for them.No one wants to serve someone else,they are just helpless and After all,from humans,humanity must be expected."

She is done with her cleaning and after saying this she just passes by me.Did this timid,polite girl just call me inhuman.Seems like,she does have a voice after all.

She is intriguing and she is interesting me more than she should.

1.Do you like the chapter?

2.What are your thoughts about Iana,Aiden and Ehan??

Vote and comment.

Untill next time,

Astral

Chapter 5:Stolen moments

A FEW MONTHS LATER

EHAN'S POV:

In this world everyone is an open book but you need to know the language to read them and some of them are written in a rare language.But no matter how rare it is,there are always some people who can read them thoroughly and speak their language fluently.

Iana is written in one of those rare languages.Shy and introverted. self contained.It's hard to miss how her hands fist her dress when she meets someone new.How less she let's strangers see her.

The moon illuminates her face just enough and the breeze caresses her so gently as if it is scared of hurting her.She looks like the first time I had seen her,the prettiest portrait but the only difference is that,at that time she was nothing to me and now she is everything to me.

In these few months I am still just a stranger to her but she has become so much more to me,the most important to me.Seeing her so often,observing her,made me love her all the more,Her calm auro,observent personality,everything entices me.

Sitting in front of her,seeing her sleeping figure,calms me.Deep and peaceful sleep engulfs her.She has clutched her soft toy as if her life abides in it.I really dislike that my sweetheart has decided to keep it with her that too so close,But no worries,it is only a matter of time before she learns but of course such actions would have consequences that she would have to face.

She has a long way ahead of her Because she won't be mine on her own would have to make her mine.She won't give up so easily I would have to make her. Within this short time I have realized that and reading her diary has definitely proved to be a benefit.

When I first realized my feelings I wanted to send a proposal inst antly.Seeing her often gave me peace.I visited home every week.I had gone to a business trip and I hated every moment of it.i hoped that I could bring her with me.Returning from the business trip of two weeks and I wanted to see her.It was almost 12 am.She must had to be asleep and so I went to her dorm.I had it's key for some time and as I had thought she was asleep.

She was in a very cute pair of pajamas.I couldn't help smiling to myself. I am eager to have her in my arms but I just remind myself that very soon she will be.I wanted to touch her,to hold her close to me butof course it had to wait.

It was not long before my eyes landed on her diary and I started reading it. For the most part her diary angered me.

The most unforgivable fault was that she wrote pages after pages about that "best friend" of hers. All the outings they had togethe r.This type of behavior definitely didn't suite the to be Iana Ehan Syed.Why would that boy be so close to her and why would she let him?He will die,he has to but not just now.

Reading her diary also gave me some other insights in he life which made me know that she would never say yes to this marriage and like previously mentioned I would have to make her.

She has mentioned in her diary that marriage for her is a wish not a want and so is love because she doesn't think she would find someone,respectful,kind,easy-going.

It is evident that she will never marry a leader of an organized crime syndicate(Mafia).Her life goals are literally-religion, passion and helping everyone and for the last one she is even working with that bastard on a project regarding an NGO and she would loath me along with everyone in this family if she came to know about it.

That's why I had to be patient but just because I was patient doesn't mean I have forgotten about her mistakes. She will have to pay for every single one of them when it is time. And now that all the preparations are done that isn't very far either. Because soon she will be IANA EHAN SYED, my wife.

She will be by my side, her rightful place and she has to accept it whether she wants it or not. If she accepts it easily It would be easier for her but if she doesn't she will just make things hard for her. But irrespective of what she does the end result would be the same and that is in my arm.her destination is me but the path is up to her.

If you are confused about any part of this chapter,feel free to ask me questions.

VOTE AND COMMENT.

1.What are your thoughts about this chapter?

2.What do you think of Ehan?

3.Does this seem too abrupt?

Until next time

Astral

Chapter 6:Letting someone in

ANA'S POV:

Serene is the best word to describe the scene in front of me.It truly is serene.away from this chaotic world.We are on a mountain top,me and Aiden.It has been a few months from the last meteor shower with everyone..Allah knows if I would ever enter jannat(Heaven) but if not this is the closest I can get to that.

Tonight instead of going to the library we decided to come here.T his place kind of revives me.I have so many memories with this place.

Almost two years ago was the first time I came here.It was my birthday.

Flashback:

My ringtone snaps me out of my thoughts.It's Zer.I receive the call and we exchange salam.

"Hey,can you come to the uni entrance?"He asks me.

"Why?Aren't we going to the library today?"I cannot help asking.

"Just come here,pleaseeeeee.."He insists.

"Okay,I will be there in a minute."I reply.

After waking up and getting ready,I was headed to the library like we always do.But looks like something came up.

When I reach the entrance,I see him there with his car.

Before I can say something,he says,"please get in your highness"With a bow.

"where are we going,that too so late at night."I ask him.I am also a bit hesitant.i have never done something like this and I never had a male friend.

He realizes my discomfort and says,"Iana,do you trust me?"A simple question but in most cases paired with a complicated answer but not for me because I do trust him and I also know that he can never harm me.So,I get in,a token of my trust.

We drive for sometime until we have reached a mountain and then he gets out.I follow his lead.The sight that I am met with after I get out is beyond beautiful.Stars above me mesmerizes me whereas the soft grass beneath my now bare feet provide a unique comfort.

When I look back at him,he is standing there with a cake and a gift."Happy birthday to purest soul on this planet."He wishes me.

"Can this day be any more amazing!"I exclaim.

"Wait for it.This is just the beginning."He says.

We cut the cake of which we eat less and smear more on each others face.We both look like cartoons before cleaning up.Then I open my gift accompanied by a beautiful card.There is a cute backpack and in it there is a stitch soft toy.

The card said,

Happy Birthday.May happiness be your eternal companion and sadness not even a temporary one.May you reach the highest summit and beyond because even the highest one is short in comparison to your capabilities and may our friendship last forever and one day because I don't want it to end even after forever.

Your best friend

Zer

"There is a mistake in it",I say suddenly.

"what is it?"he asks me not able to figure out what went wrong.

"See,here you were supposed to write annoying but you wrote best",I say like like i am pointing it out to a child and trying to suppress my laugh.

He gives me a look which says seriously and says,"I am offende."

After calmimg down a bit I say,"sorry,this is just amazing.better than amazing."

"apology accepted"he says trying to be serious but then we both end up laughing again.

We see the sunrise from there and then we leave for another "surprise", according to him.when we reach there,I find out we are there for squba diving.Not in my wildest dream had I thought that and It was so much fun.It was just so colourful and lively,full of life and beauty.beautiful is an understatement for that day and it was all the more beautiful because it was with him.We stayed there for a long time.Both of us had a lot of fun.

At night we go to a café and grab dinner."THis was the best birth-day I have ever had.So,thank you."I say.

"You deserve it."He says accompanied by a smile.

End of flashback

At that time I had no idea that his gift,stitch soft toy foreshadowed a event.Because he did find me lost and broken and he did put me together.(There is a movie lilo and stitch and stich is a character of that movie and lilo and stitch means lost and put back together in Hawaiian)

"What would I do without you"I say

"Guess,we will never find out.I will always be there to annoy you ."he says while poking my head and I whine because he always does that.

"Now I am starting to think I would be better without you"I huff.

He looks straight into my eyes and says,"hey,That's not happenin g.We are best friends and Even death can't do us part.I will follow you irrespective of heaven or hell."

"So will I"I reply with a smile.

"even if I don't find heaven...."He starts the sentence.

ZER'S POV:

"I will walk through hell with you"She ends it.

It's our thing.We had first started it at this very place.

Flashback:

"Hey.Iana,can you pass me that book"I whisper to her because we are in the library.When she extends her hand to pass me the book her dress travels up her forearm and something catches my eye.A scar,self harm scar,It is not new but still visible.Her eyes travel to where my eyes are fixed and within a moment she hides her hand.

The rest of the day she hardly talks to me and not for once does she look me in the eye.From when I met iana there were these periods where she wouls be silent,by that I don't mean not speaking,i mean her whole personality dying down but sahe would come around again.I didn't know what to make of it but now I know that something is definitely wrong.

"Hey let's go to the mountain,okay?" and we got to our spot.The mountain.

When we reace there it is as beautiful as always.Wrapped in a shawl of silence,enclosed with beauty and that beauty complemented by the comfort and familiar feeling it provided.We sit there for a long time before I finally ask her,"Iana,How are you?"

A simple question but it's answer far more complicated.She doesn't say anything.Probably confused about what to say.But she is in pain and as a withness to that tears makes their way out.I can't express how I feel through words.My heart breaks into pieces seeing her tears.

When she doesn't reply for a few momments I just say,"Iana I can't force you but I am requesting you.You have no idea how much you mean to me and I can,t see you like this.I can't let you go on like this even after knowing that you are in pain."

She just looks at me and she perhaps sees the care.That I care for her,more than anything and she let's me see her other side.The side which is broken.She starts,"My sister had a abusive tendency,not beause she is evil or anything but.....it was almost like a split personality disorder.You won't be able to recognize the other person. Sometimes it was just too much to bear and at one point I started cutting myself.It took away that overwhelming feeling that frustrat ion.Whenever I would look at a knife my mind would whisper "slash your wrist or stab yourself."When ever I would look down from a roof,it would say,"Come on,jump"It is almost like a reverie,hard to break out from in that moment.My relationship with my sister have improved so much but my mind just doesn't stop doing these.When even the smallest things happen out of my control,I slip away in that same thing.".

I let her cry her heart out.Who knows how long she has been bottling her emotions for and she need to get it out.Then I just say as softly as possible"Iana.look at me" and she looks up at me and I continue my sentence,"and listen to me carefully,I will always be there for you,even if no one is.Your childhood was definitely not pretty and it'd their fault.it's their loss.You are not the one at fault.You are the one who suffered and I promise that this will pass.we will make it pass.

I promise even if we don't find heaven I will walk through hell with you.You are not alone because I am gonna stand by you."

End of flashback

I wanted her to see a psychiatrist.I wanted her to be free from this burden but she didn't wanna talk to a stranger about her issues.But,I was not a stranger and she could talk to me and to be better equipped I started studying psychology most of my time even at night.Started taking online courses and all.But suddenly Iana changed her mind and she wanted to go to psychiatrist and I took her to a familiar doctor of our family.She liked the doctor.I drove her there for every session though she always said that there was no need.But I wanted to be there for her.

Later on when I had asked her what made her change her mind her answer was,"Your grades were decreasing,you always looked sick and tired and yet somehow you suddenly knew a lot about psychology. How Could I not?"Untill that point I never thought that she knew.

Now when I am here with her,I am grateful that I found out because she is so much better.She is......fine and I couldn't be happier.

P.S-not edited

Again,feel free to point out mistakes.The next chapter would be Ehan's pov.

1.I wanted to give a insight into Iana and Zer's life.What do you think about it?

2.What are your thoughts about Iana and Zer?

Please vote and comment.

Untill next time,

Astral

chapter 7:Done waiting

E HAN'S POV:

Another weekend that I decided to stay in syed mansion,i think as my car rolls in the driveway..I have my own mansion which I prefer because of the isolation it provides as well as the privacy it accommodates but these few months I have been coming here every weekend because of a certain someone.

Seeing her in front of me gives peace.I have eyes on her every second of the day and pretty often I go to her dorm at night but there is a difference between seeing her sleep and seeing her awake.,though I love both equally.

Being emerged in my thoughts I reach my room which is in the opposite wing in the house on second floor along with being sound-proof.i wish I could go into her room right now,see her and hold her close but that would just give her a bad impression and I don't want that of course,unless she forces me to.

For her my one side is reserved.She doesn't need to know that I lead a organized crime syndicate,that it is a family business.That the family she thinks is a saint is far more sinister.That Ibrahim and Hanan both are involved in it though much less and they take care of the legal side more.

I shake off these thoughts fast because otherwise I would end up in her room before I can stop myself with a promise that she will be in front of my eyes tomorrow morning.

Sitting at the dining table for breakfast,the one that I am waiting for doesn't come.I am very interested in knowing what or who came in her way.Now breakfast seems more like a burden then a wish and I get over with it as fast as I can.

I could leave the table but I don't want anyone to know about things before I want then to but I am pretty sure Mom knows.I can see it in her eyes.

after returning to my study the first thing I do is make a call,"Where is Iana?"

"Sir,she is with Aiden."

My hand tightens on the phone on it's own.I have a great control over my body but it is in case of her where I lose control.My hayati is yet to learn but she will soon.

"Where?"

"Sir,it is on of their regular outings which started with a cycling."

I cut the call that moment.I know what I need to know.Her mental health was the only thing stopping me from doing something because I didn't want her t deteriot but now I don't see any reason to hold back anymore.

She is much better and she needs to understand her place.She needs to take it and it is right beside me.I have given her more than enough time but it is over now.

Iana's calm collected self has always infatuated me.Even in a loud atmosphere she would be quite,tucked in a corner,enjoying that loudness without necessarily joining it.

There were a very few people that she is comfortable with and I can see that.Moreovrer,she is such a responsible girl.She knows what is expected of her and can shoulder it without as much as an excuse.

I love her and I would have her irrespective of how many things I have to fix or change about her.How much I have to train her but it makes me happy that there isn't much on the list.

The only thing that I found bad was this friendship with this guy.But she is young and some mistakes must be made allownce for,not forgiven but let pass until she knows better,until I make her know better.But she could stop digging her grave now because she has already dug enough with this one single mistake.

I know that this bastard is just a friend to her because if he had been anything more than he would not have lived to see this day but yet she I don't want her having friends like this one as well.She doesn't need them.

I am done waiting.I would talk to Dadaji about this proposal and he would talk to Hayati about it.I already know how this is gonna go and everything is already in place for that exact purpose but I do hope she says yes for her sake.

it is true that I will break my beloved but I will not let her stay broken.I will put all the pieces back inot place the way I like.After all it is for her and she will warm up to me sometime.She hast to.

If need be I will cut her off from every single person of the rest of the world,literally.,I will take her to one of my islands or in one of the mansions surrounded by forest so that there is none between us.The only human connection she feels is with me.She has to accept me,submit to me and she will.

1.Do you find Ehan twisted?

2.Do you think that Iana will submit or will she fight back?

Untill next time,

Astral

Chapter 8:Sudden proposal

- -

This chapter is dedicated to ,one of my very first readers who didn't give up on me and ,a friend and a loyal reader.

EHAN'S POV:

I came home today to talk to Dadaji about Iana.I enter his room after knocking and taking permission.I take a seat and without beating around the bush I say,"Hume apse kuch bat karni thi."(I wanted to talk to you about something.)

"Batao,"he tells me to go on.(Ok.)

"Hum bat ko nahi ghumaenge.Hume Iana pasand hei.Hum nikah karna chahte hei Iana se aur hum chahte hei ke ap usse is bari mei bat kare."I say straight up.(I won't beat around the bush.I like Iana and I want you to talk to her about it.)

After a moment he tells me,"Bhul jao use."(Forget her,)

I knew that he wouldn't be happy with it because Iana holds a special place in his heart as he sees Aabroo fupi in her.But I didn't think that he would straight up deny me.

"Ap bhi jante hei ki asa nahi ho sakta."I state the obvious.(Even you know thar it is not possible.)

"Tumse bohat choti ha woh aur tumhare sath adjust bhi nahi kar payegi.Tumhare tor tarike use mar dalenge."(She is much younger than you and she won't be able to adjust with you.Your ways would kill her.)

"Iana ko adjust karwana meri jimadari hei aur apke tor tariko ne toh dadiji ko nahi mar dala nahi baba ke ammi ko."(I would make sure that she adjusts and your ways didn't kill grandma neither did baba's kill Ammi.)I paused for a moment before continuing."Agar ap usse nahi bat karte hei toh me..."(If you don't talk to her then I....)

Before I could even finish the sentence he interrupted me with,"Tum asa kuch bhi nahi karoge.Mei usse bat karta hei par tum itna wada karo ki agar woh na kahe to tum use force nahi karoge."He said.(You won't do anything like that but promise me if she says no then you are not gonna force her.)

"Mei sirf itna hi keh sakta ho ki mei use tabtak shakti se nahi peshaunga jabtak jarurat pare."After saying this I took my leave and left.(I can only say that I won't force her until needed.)

I never saw her because Aabroo committed suicide and died at a young age but by what I have heard from baba dadaji loved her more then anyone else.After three sons she was born,his beloved daughter.For everyone he was a strict person.For his sons he was a father but also the leader of a organized crime syndicate but for her he was just a father.

Her death completely crushed him and you ca still see tears in his eyes when he talks about her and because of something he sees her in Iana.That is one of the reasons why she become so close with this family so fast.Despite having three grand daughters it was Iana he saw her in.

IANA'S POV:

Yesterday something completely unexpected happened.It was more than unexpected.it was kind of a shock.

Yesterday I was at syed mansion.We just had dinner and went to the movie room when a maid told me that Dadaji had asked for me.I didn't have the slightest idea what it was for but I went nevertheless. When I reached his room I knocked first and after hearing a faint come in,I entered the room.

I went inside and took a seat on the couch,opposit to Dadaji.I sat with my eyes on my lap waiting for Dadaji to say what he wanted to say.

"Iana,bete,kasi ho.Parhai kasi chal rahi hei."He at first asked me.(Iana,dear how are you?How is your studies going?)

"Ji,thik ho aur parhai bhi thik hi chal rahi hai."(I am fine and studies are going on pretty good,)

""Iana,bete hume apse kuch bat karni thi.Ap ei mut soche ki hum apper dabab dalna chahte hei.Hum bas apse puchna chahte hei aur ap soch kar hume jabab dijiye ga."(I want to talk to you about so mething.Don't think that I am pressurizing you.I just want to ask you and and I want you to think about it and tell me what you truly want.)

"Ji,"I nod my head.(Ok)

"Apko ai sab bohat hi achanak lag sakta hei par hum kafi dino se apke sath is bari mei bat karna chah rehe the.Bete hum apko Ehan ki liye bohat pasand karte hei aur hum Ehan ki liye apka hath mangna chahte hei.Kya ap is rishte se khush hongi?"(You might find all this very abruot but I wanted to talk to you about these for a few dats.I think you are perfect for Ehan and I want you to marry him.Would you be happy with it.)

The moment his words register in my mind my eyes involuntarily travel to him.I don't know what to say and at a loss of words my mouth open and close a few times.I am completely flabbergasted.

Never in my wildest dream did I think that something like this would happen.This came as a even bigger shock because I thought Hanan api and Ehan bhaijan were supposed to get married.Everyone knows that Hanan api likes Ehan bhaijan.Then how come her own family can't see it.

Even if she didn't like him I would have still refused to marry him because though this is an wonderful family right now marriage is the last thing on my list and I don't like him.He is the opposite of what I want in my life.

Dadaji notices my lack of response as well as nervousness and says,"Bache tum pareshan kiu ho rahi ho.Agar tum abhi jabab nahi dena chahte to phir badme jabab de dena.Jab tumhe thik lage tum tab hume jabab se sakti ho." to calm me.(Bete why are you getting tensed?If you don't wanna reply now then reply later.You can tell me about your decision whenever you are ready,)

At this point I pull myself together and finally answer his question,"Nahi,dadaji,bakt ki koi jarurat nahi he."(NO

"kya yahi apka finale decision he."(Is this your final decision.)

"Ji.Ap naraz hua kya mujhse?"I question looking at him.(Yes.Did I make you angry?)

"Nahi bete,bilkul nahi."He says.(No,bete,not at all.)

After waiting a moment I ask for permission to leave and after receiving that I get up to leave.

On the doorstep I stop for moment contemplating whether I should tell him about Hanan but decide against it because it's not my matter.But I do feel bad for her.

Seeing me stop on the doorstep Dadaji asks me,"Kuch aur kehna chahte hei?"(Do you wanna say something else?)

"Ji nahi,bilkul nahi."(No,not at all)I say and head outside.I don't feel like watching a movie now but they are waiting for me.So,it would be really rude to not go.I go there and sit throughout the movie without particularly catching anything or any part of it.

After the movie is finished we just head to our rooms.Just when I lock my door and sit on the bed there is a knock.After opening the door I see that it is Ayesha and Humaira and after entering and making themselves comfortable on my bed,Ayesha asks me,"Iana,kya hua hai tumhe.Itni khoi khoi kyu ho."(Iana.what happened.Why are you so lost?)

I don't know why but I just feel like telling them about it and I do.I feel like they should know about it.

Right that moment Hanan api enters the room as she had gone for some snacks and asks me,"Are,kya bat horahi hei mere bina?"(Hey,what are you talking about without me?)

We don't mention anything to her because I am pretty sure she would feel really bad if she came to know.She really likes him.You can see it in her eyes.

Fupi-Father's sister

bete-daughter,an endearment

Baba-father

Ammi-mother

Dadaji-grandfather

I updated after a very long time and I am so sorry for that.I wanted to update after this story crossed 1k reads but within the meantime it crossed 1.5 k reads and 222 votes.

I am sincerely grateful to every single one of you for giving this story a chance.Thank you.

Vote and comment.

1.What do you think about this chapter?Tell me in the comment section.

Until next time,Astral

Chapter 9:Consequences

IANA'S POV:

After breakfast I take my leave from syed Mansion and after finishing my classes go to the book store where I work.It's a peaceful job and for the most part and you can study here.

After coming here my parents insisted several times to pay for all of my expenses but I wanted to be independent.Be truly indepent and so I got a job so that I could pay for my own expenses.Living off their money and chanting about independence would be hypocrisy.

After returning to my dorm at night I follow my daily routine.Just when I am about to go to sleep I receive a call from Abbu.

"Assalwalikum abbu,,"I say after receiving.(Assalwalikum,father,)-abbu means father.

"Walikum assalam,ma.Kemon acho."He asks me.(walaikum assal am,ma.How are you?)-Ma is used as an endearment.It's literal meaning is mother.

"Ji abbu valo achi.Tumi?"(I am fine abbu.How are you?)

"Amio valo achi.Tomar poralekha Kemon choltese?"(I am fine to o.How are your studies going?)

"Alhamdulillah.Abbu araf Kemon ache?"I ask about my brother and after talking to my brother for a few minutes I hang up.(Alham dullial.Abbu how is araf?)

Abbu has always been an extremely supportive person in my life .When I wanted to come to abroad for my studies it was abbu who supported me.Otherwise My apu and ammu were strictly against it.

To be truthful, we don't talk that much but yet he is my ideal and I Love him more than anything and my brother,well I am like a second mother to him.I would go through a hundred difficulties before letting any reach him.

After talking to them I go to sleep.

There is a rhythmic sound around me and it awakens me.I sit up.Then I wake up or I don't.I am not sure whether this is a dream or a reality.It's dark around me it takes me a few seconds to adapt to the moonlight swarming the room.But it's still scarce.Now I notice a man at the opposite side of the room,sitting on a sofa,making that rhythmic sound with his gun,tapping it on the table.

Something prickes my eyes,my vision becomes blurry.It's tears.The first thought that crosses my mind is that I have been trafficked and now they are gonna sell me.But I force myself to get over that fear and anxiousness and think.This is not the time to lose myself.

I notice my surroundings,as much can be noticed that,I am on a bed which feels very comfortable as well as the fact that I am the only girl in this room.The room is well furnished.If I had been trafficked then I probably would have been in a cage with many other girls.But I am not which makes it unlikely that I have been trafficked .

It doesn't seem plausible that I am already sold because my cloths are the one that I was wearing.there is also a additional hijab on my head.

Yet that burden is not lifted off my chest.This silence,his calm calculating state is weighing down on me.His observant eyes making me aware of my every nerve ending.My body sensitive even to the breeze,my eyes fixated on him,scared to even blink unware what the next frame would bring.

Why is he sitting there like a statue.I wanna make a dash for the dooor but he has a gun and I am pretty sure the door is locked.

Now he gets up from where he was sitting and comes to me, right in front of me and sit on the bed.Every part of my body feels like water the moment I see him.it's like I lose control of my limbs.It's Ehan Syed.A thousand thoughts cloud my mind rendering it incapable of holding onto any of them.Among all this a single word leaves my mouth,"Why?"

"Finally awake,hayati,"He says.Not finding it necessary to answer my question.His endearment,hayati meaning my life kind of throws me off.

"Where am I?Why have you bought me here?please.."Before I can complete my sentence he interrupts me.

"You know,hayati,Every action has some consequences.So,we should think before we take any decision."He pauses and looks at me,his eyes sharp,"But you didn't.When you were asked to marry me you said NO."

"you should have thought,hayati,before doing so."He tsks,"Now some people who are very close to you will pay for a mistake they never committed."

"What are you going to do?"I can't help asking.

"You will soon find out."he says,his tone edgy,I suddenly notice that my palm are sweaty and clammy in a air conditioned room.

The only coherent thought right now reining my mind is this is insane.HE IS INSANE.

"You are doing all this because I refused to marry you!"my voice incredulous."What would you get by forcing me.I would never love you."

His eyes turn sinister and he clicks his tongue,"You will learn to love me."He says nonchalantly.

"I would rather di....."

"DON'T YOU DARE FINISH THAT SENTENCE."He yells,his voice booming in the room.I visibly flinch,tears clouding my vision.My father or any other male in my life had never even screamed at me.

My tear stained face softens his features."You don't have the permission to even think about that,"He says while trying to wipe my tears but I pull back.His hands stop midair and the moment I do so,his expression changes.He chuckles to himself.It mockes me,tells me to look around myself and see who is in charge.

"I can do a lot more if I want,hayati,don't tempt me."He warns me.His warning visibly shakens me.Making me aware of my surroundings once more.

Then when he came to wipe my tears I don't pull myself back.I am desperate to get out of here and I will play by his rules unless they don't harm me.

He could do anything and no one would find out.He has a gun.It is best for me to not make him angry and get out of this situation which I have no idea now I landed myself into and then do something.Any harsh steps would be foolish.I haven't been here for half an hour and his bipolarity is already scaring me.His indifferent attitude sickening.

Ya Allah,what even is this!A nightmare or reality and how in the absolute hell did I land myself in it.

"Why are you doing all this?"I again ask him.

"To make sure that the next time you are asked you don't have the audacity to say no."He says as calmly as a summer noon but containing equal intensity.

"you haven't met me properly or talked to me once.You don't know me.I could turn out much worse then your expectation.Why gamble like this?"I try to reason more like manipulate him.

He coaks an eyebrow at my effort before saying"I know you more than you know yourself and you can't manipulate."

You are insane.What would your family think when they come to know about this.Moreover Hanan loves you.Why don't you marry her-I wanna scream at him.But I don't.There is no use reasoning with someone like this.He didn't think twice before kidnapping someone who is very close to his family.Allah knows what are his limits.

"You can't do this,"I state firmly,faking confidence.

"You sure,hayati,"he mocks me.

His attitude is testing my patience.I feel like I wanna punch him in the face but I just glare at him.

"Let's see where is this attitude of yours by tomorrow,"He pauses and leans in before continuing, "Because tomorrow is gonna bring an absolute havoc."

I smell somethink and darkness engulfs while my mind fights with itself to stay awake,to figure out his intentions.Not let my life crumble apar........

I feel something warm and bright on my face.All on a sudden last night washes over me like a shockwave and I sit up right away.It's morning,5 a.m.Was it true or was it just a dream.I tell myself that it was just a nightmare. That someone from that family would never do something like that to me.But deep down I know that it wasn't.Oth erwise it's not possible for me to wake up so late.Even if I had turned off the alarm I would have remembered doing it.But I don't.Yet,I shut my heart off.

But the problem is how do I make others believe it was real and not a dream.What prove do I have.They would think of me as crazy.

That's when it hits me that Aiden must be waiting and worried about me.I check my phone to see 67 missed calls,one just 5 minutes before.Ya Allah,help me from his wrath.That's when I receive another call and I take it,"Hello,Aiden.."

He lets out a shaky breath,it's every bit washed with relief"Are you fine,"he asks me.

I want to tell him.I don't have to fear that he won't believe it because he will.But not on a call especially when he is already worried.

"Yep."

"Ok,ok,ok.You are ok.Everything is ok."

"I am sorry,Please forgive me."I feel really guilty for making him worry so much.

"You have to treat me to sandwich in he canteen then I would ....think about it."

A involuntary smile adorns my face mirroring his from the opposite side,"Ok,After third class."

Then we hang up.I make myself believe that this day is just like any other and nothing happened.that he is there and he would help me even if something happens.

Suddenly I have caught cold.It is not probably not corona but still it's irritating.Pray for me.

requested an update and some requests must be fulfilled. So,here it is.

Can I please get 30 votes and 20 comments.

1.What are your thoughts about this chapter?Tell me in the comments.

2.What do you think about this endearment Hayati.It's an Arabic endearment which means my life.

Untill next time,

Astral

Chapter 10:Frozen

Happy Victory Day,Everyone.

Long chapter ahead,1564.

IANA'S POV:

"I am not sure but something happened last night,"I say confused.

Within a moment his whole demeanor changes.Gone is the joking,carefree side.We are where we always are,you guessed it,the library and I had to tell him what happened.

"What?"He says urging me to go on.

Right that moment my cell vibrates,indicating a call.It's my father and After telling Aiden to wait a minute,I receive the call with,"Assalwalaikum,abbu."

"Walaikum assalam."His reply is almost a whisper.His voice strained like something very bad happened and he is dreading even telling me about it.

"Kmon acho ma?"It's like he is trying to ease me before breaking the news.(How are you,dear?)

"Abbu ki hoiche?"I can't help questioning.This silence is killing me.(Abbu,what happened?)

He sighs and then speaks,"Shodhomatro ekta kotha mone rakhba je sob thik hoi jabe ar tension koreo na.Ami tomake boltam na kintu na bolle hoito tumi anno kothao theke ata Shonta."(Just remember that everything would be fine and don't be tensed.Iwouldn't have told you but if I didn't you probably would have heard it from somewhere else.)

"Abbu,ki hoiche.Please,bolo."(Abbu,what happened,please,telll me.)

"Police arrested Araf for possession of drugs,"

"he was taking drugs,"i whisper before I can stop myself.More to myself then to him.This just cannot be.

"And selling them,apparently,"He adds.

"He is still in jail.!Abbu,when was he arrested?"I ask almost pan-icked.

"A few hours prior,"

"Abbu,hire a lawyer and apply for bail.He is just 15."

"It's thrusday night.The counrts are closed.We cannot apply for a bail until Monday,"He sighs and it is enough to tell me hoe much he tried.

"Right this moment I hear my mother's voice from background and my father instantly cuts the call so that it doesn't reach me but he is a second too late and her broken voice,laced with worry and concern frightens me.

I had come out of the library to talk to him and now Aiden walks out for me.I needed to return to my dorm.I couldn't bear to be there a second longer and I refuse to let my brain think it over before I am in the safe confines of my room.Today,Aiden follows me inside,the first time he does so.

After I sit down on my bed this hits me for the first time.Araf is taking drugs....and selling them!Araf!The most well behaved boy I have ever seen and what did he need that we didn't give him that he had to sell them.My brother became addicted at 15 and I wasn't there to see the symptoms.neither was I there to stop it.

In a moment anger,anger for none but myself takes over me.He is a kid.he is supposed to make mistakes but I should have been there to guide him.I prioritized myself over my little brother.When I look at Aiden,his look tells me exactly what I look like but I don't need it to tell me.i know what I look like.Eyes bloodshot red,anger radiating from every feature.

Without wasting another moment I book a ticket for this afternoon.

"Aiden,i need to go home.Araf was found with drugs and he was arrested.i need to be there for my father and for him."

Within a second his face goes from surprised to shocked to supportive.

"I will drop you and I am sure the professors would understand. After all,this ia an emergency."

He leaves to give me the privacy to pack.I even realise after he is gone.I pack as fast as I can,freshen up,collect my papers,checking and rechecking them to make sure they are ok and leave because It would take a bit to get to the Airport and The traffic is uncontrolleble.

"Araf has an amazing sister and it's okay to derail,we all do but I know that you would make sure that he is fine"He tells me right before I enter the airport.

I had called my father when I was in the car and he insisted agin and again that it was not needed.I know that he didn't want me to see Araf in that condition but he needs to understand that it is Araf we are talking about.My baby brother and i don't want him to go through it all now.he deserves to rest.Nt run errands to the police.After I told him that I had booked the flights he just said a defeated okay and be safe.

During boarding the officers check my papers again and again and finally tell me to step out.I don't argue because I am not in the state to.I just figure out that I am wearing hijab and moreover II look like I went through hell so it was bound to happen and they would let me out shortly.

Anyway,I am proved wrong when I sit alone in that room for hours until finally my plane takes off.My countless questions are just met with a cold shoulder like they don't even hear me until finally exhausted I just sit down and wait for whatever is bound to happen.I am too worried to care for whatever is happening to me and I will be fine because I haven't done anything.

I am sitting with my face buried in my hands when someone enters the room for the umpteenth time and I can bet that even they would get whatever is necessary for their work and leave.So,I don't bother looking up until that person comes and sits on the chair beside mine.Too close for my liking.When I do look up,it doesn't take me even a moment to realize or more like be sure that he did this.

"You did it,didn't you?"I say more like a statement then a questio n.My face sharp void of any emotion.

"You made me do it,Hayati,"He says like it is a valid enough reaso n.like I had begged him to do it.Forced him.

"Just this?"I ask and I think he knows what I am pointing at.It's not that I didn't consider that possibility but how could he is beyond me.Bangladesh is literally on opposite part of the world and how did he get his hands on drugs and how did he find them out of 16 crore people.

"You are smart,aren't you?"He said which meant if you are smart enough then you know it.

"Quit it,Mr. syed.I am nothing to you and neither will I ever be."

"Last night you were sure that I couldn't do anything yet here we are"He states followed by a smile which literally burns my blood.Si ckeningly sweet.

"How can you do this!"I whisper barely audible to my own ears. My eyes land straight on his,holding his accountable while I repeat myself,"How could you do it!I looked at you as nothing but an elder brother.I am 8 years younger than you.How could you even think about this.This is absolutely disg............"Before I could even complete my sentrence,within a literal split second,his hand travel to the back of my neck and his face stop at inches away from mine.The change was too fast to be able to react.At first he was saying hmm with my reasonings as nonchalant as ever,Then,boom!

"Don't you dare call our relationship names.You are already in hot water,don't put yourself in more."He seethes.Anger underlying his statement.

I was startled to say the least and then angry.

"Don't.Touch.Me."I seeth with equal intensity.My sentence is hardly complete when his lips crash with mine.I am too shocked for the initial seconds to even figure out and he taking advantage of this shock explore my mouth.When I do get out of this shock survival instincts kick in. I try to push him with as much force as I can. when I do so his free hand gets hold of both of mine and he holds them behind me while his other hand maneuvers my face according to his liking because I had started moving my face to get out.

I just want to get out of this situation.I desperately do.It is making me feel disgusting like never before and I could give anything at this moment to get out.I wanna rip my own face off.The first 2 tears make their way out of both my eyes.

When he was done,his lips left mine and his face rested beside mine while he whispered in my ears,"And I kissed you.What are you gonna do about that."alluding to my previous statement-don't touch me.

The moment his hands left me I stumbled backwards,my chair fell with a thud.My legs carried themselves to the wall behind me for some kind of support.He gets up and comes and stands right in front of me.He lowers his face so that he can look me in the eye because I won't and continues ,"And I could make love to you right here,right now,would you be able to do anything about that?"

"I own you more then you own yourself so,don't tell me whether I can touch you."After this statement I look right at him.I feel......sho cked.I have quite sincerely lost my voice because.I can't get one word out of my mouth.

Now he presses me to the wall and his forhead rests on mine.He wipes my eyes with the pad of his thumb and says"I love you a lot Iana.Your every wish would be my command.Accept my love and it would be easier for everybody because otherwise I would have to make you."His voice so much softer,different from before.Like he is talking to a child.Like,he didn't just threaten to rape me.

In times of danger it is always flight or fight but another thing that happens all too often is:freeze.I am frozen, still.Very few times in my life I had no idea,no plan about what to do and now is one of them.

"I will not hurt you,"He starts and then looking at me adds almost as an afterthought "Physically,but sadly your loved ones don't fall in the criteria."_____

_____

P.S:not edited

Vote and Comment.

I am back after a very long time and forgive me for that.Those of you who read from the very beginning know that there is a chapter about meteor shower and I am thinking about replacing it with another one.I was very excited about meteor shower in that time and so wrote a chapter.

1.What do you think Iana will do?2.What are your thoughts about everything Ehan did?

Untill next time,

Astral

Chapter 11:Betrayal

This chapter is dedicated to
_____

When you are messing with a part of someone's life,you are messing with their entire life.   Hannah baker,13 reasons why

IANA'S POV:

"All of this can stop,right this moment,all I need is one word from you,"He says as softly as a breeze while still stroking my face.

"But you are 8 years older than me,"the words escape me.Within this short time of that proposal and now so much has happened.He has done so many things which one wouldn't want in a future partner and let's be honest I didn't want him even before that.

But discarding every single one of them,what I do point out is,his age.A inconsequential detail.When you break a big news to a child, like say their parents are getting divorced and they being naïve don't really know what to say to stop.

Like what would be big enough problem to stand in the way of that divorce.So they grab at whatever they can at their disposal to try,something like but how is my goldfish gonna live in 2 houses.So mehow,my question seemed to fall in that category.

"Does that seem like such a big thing,"i can feel him smiling while saying that. But I said that in a state of despair, To hold onto anything at my disposal.

"But I don't want you...."I can hear myself whisper. Now I am truly not even talking to him because I figured out that he is not someone who can be reasoned with.

"So, who else do you want?" His voice turns a lot darker,edgier than before." Hmm?"

All on a sudden, he takes a step back from me and I finally feel like I can breath. I finally stop trying to merge with the wall.

He upright the chair that I had knocked and sits on it, facing me. His right ankle resting on his left knee.

"Still not done with this game, are we?" He mocks me.

"You will be soon," He says a lot more darkly.LIke a promise.

"You don't wanna marry me,huh?The next time we meet you will beg me to marry you."He spats.

"The airport security would let you go but don't try to leave this country again," After saying this he gets up to leave but pauses right at the door and calls out," You might wanna call home after you get out of here. Who knows what other disaster has befallen them," and leaves.

His touch still lingers on my skin, his voice still rings in my ear and his threat still keeps gnawing at me. My body slides down the wall on it's own and all I wanna do now is just break down. But right now I don't have the luxury to fall apart. Not when my baby brother is in jail because of me.

Think, what now. What do you wanna do now. Who is gonna be helpful. Whom to approach. Come on, think I say out loud forcing myself to make a plan.

okay,here is what you are gonna do.You are gonna go to syed mansion and ask Dadaji for help.But how are you gonna get there?It's 11p.m.You are gonna book a uber,I keep talking to myself so that I can do what I need to and not fall in a trance. So that, i don't think about how ridiculous all this is.

I book a uber and it soon arrives. After I get into it the first thing I do is call home and they don't receive it. None does.Worry clutches me and my mind keeps visiting his threat.

Suddenly the uber halts and I realize that I have reached syed mansion. I was so engrossed in reaching home that I wasn't even aware of my surroundings.

It is only after reaching that I think it is pretty late and Dadaji might not be awake.But I need him to be awake,my mind whispers.

Within seconds I find myself in front of his room,everybody was probably in the lounge but I didn't even notice.

The lights are on and relief washes over me.All this can finally end.He would listen to his grandfather....,right?I find myself asking.

After 2 knocks and a come in,I enter,Right when Dadaji's eyes land on me,worry engulfs them and he asks me right away,"Bete kya hua?"(Dear,what is wrong?)

He is sitting on the sofa and I go and sit at his feet.Within seconds of placing my head on his lap,I finally break down.The dam has broken and he lets me cry while stroking my head.

Whenever something would upset me too much or I would feel too overwhelmed I would come to him and cry just like this.It felt safe.

When I have finally calmed down enough to talk I start while hiccupping,"Eh-han bh-haij-jan,wo-woh ham-me for-rc-ce karr-rehe ha-ain."(Eh-han bh-hai-jan,h-he is for-rci-ng m-me.)

Within seconds,I feel his whole demeanor shift."Kya kiya he usne,"he grits.It's as if he is already angry at him.(What did he do?)

"He got Araf arrested.He stopped me at the custom and he threatened me to marry him."My voice breaks at the last sentence.This is humiliating and I want earth to swallow me whole.

"Apne to wadah kiya tha ki koi hame force nahi karega to phir woh asa kiu kar rehe hein?"I ask him while I finally look up at him.(You had promised me that none was gonna force me then why is he doing this?)

He curses under his breath before he finally turns his eyes to me and says soothingly,"Bete hume varosa karti ho?"(My child,do you trust me.)

I nod my head.

"To phir ye ayad rakho ki hum tumhe kuch nahi hone denge,"he says and pats my head while getting up.(Then remember that I won't let anything happen to you.)

He takes his phone and heads to his study.After which a almost 40 minutes screaming math ensues and it ends with Ehan bhaijan,I shouldn't call that awful person bhaijan now,cuts the call and I hear Dadaji saying his name a few more time,probably shocked that he cut the call.

I could only hear bits and pieces and it didn't sound good based on that.I can feel tears prickle at my vision again.

Finally when Dadaji enters the first thing I ask is,"Woh nehi mane?"

I can hear him sigh but he doesn't answer me and takes his previous seat.I am still where I was.

He thinks for a few moments before finally saying,"Bete,Ehan se shadi kar lo."_____

————

Vote and comment.

Let me know your thoughts in the comment section and feel free to point out mistakes.

Untill next time,Astral

Chapter 12:Plan

Finally when Dadaji enters the first thing I ask is,"Woh nehi mane?"(He didn't agree?)

I can hear him sigh but he doesn't answer me and takes his previous seat.I am still where I was.

He thinks for a few moments before finally saying,"Bete,Ehan se shadi kar lo."(marry Ehan.)

IANA'S POV:

One moment I was sitting at his feet and the next I was standing at least 10 paces away from him.My face mirrored what I felt,betrayal

"Ap asa keh bhi kese sakte hein,"I said with such hate that it visible shocked Dadaji but I couldn't help it.I was beyond angry and he was supposed to help me.....(How can you even say that?)

"Iana.bete,hum samajh sakte hein ki tum naraz ho per meri bat pehli sun lo."(Iana,dear,I can understand that you are angry but at least hear me out.)

He had hardly completed his sentence when I composed my-self,wiped my tears,exhaled in a manner people do in despair,when you have snathed away their last hope and left knowing full well that he wouldn't be able to keep up with me.He has arthritis.

I can't help bailing on conversations that I don't wanna have.Cu tting calls when I don't wanna listen to the person at the other end anymore because it does nothing other than anger me.

I walk as fast as my feet carried her.I want to leave this place as fast as I can.I can't help hating this place.It keeps playing in my head like a broken record that it wouldn't have happened if I hadn't met this family.

In this hurry to get away,I don'ty notice when I ran into Malak aunty and it was only after running into her that I see her.

"Iana.kye hua tumhe?"She asked.A look of horroe crosses her face and she starts rubbing my arm to comfort me.She drags me in a nearby room before I can protest and makes me sit.It turns out to be Ayesha's room where Humaira and Ayesha are playing video games.(Iana,what happened to you?)

She asks Ayesha to give me a glass of water and holds it to my mouth.Ayesha and Humaira seem shocked by me and I wouldn't blame them.Now they were beside me trying to comfort me.

It was only after I drink the water that she asks me,"Bache,kya hua?"(dear,what's wrong?)

I really don't wanna do this again.I doubt if they will help me.But I will try.I will knock on every door I can find.

"A few days ago Dadaji asked me if I was interested in a marriage proposal from Ehan bhaijan.I straight up refused and now
Ehan bhaijan is blackmailing me to marry him.He hurt my family."I
wrapped it as shortly as I can.

THIRD PERSON'S POV:

None of the three people that the information was disclosed to
looked shocked.Ayesha and Humaira just looked down because they
felt ashamed that they couldn't do anything.

The day Iana disclosed that she had received a proposal they knew
that it would come sooner or later.They are her friends and they are
supposed to be there for her in every pain but they can't be by her,not
in this one.

"Iana,tum ai nikah keu nahi karna chahte,"The elder women
asked,first one to break the silence.(Iana,why don't upu want this
marriage?)

Iana looked at her incredulously.Was that really the question to be
asked at that moment?

We meet a number of people before the one and we don't need a
problem with every one of them to dislike them.Sometimes,it's just
like-I don't like them.I don't feel like it with them and truly it doesn't
even matter.You are asked to make a choice and you make one and
irrespective of what it is,it should be respected.

She was aware of the look she had received in response to the
question but still went on,"Bete,give him a chance.You will like hi
m.His ways may be different but he will never hurt you."She knew

that Iana will have to agree but the faster she does the least she will suffer.(bete=dear)

At the speed of lightining Iana got up and faced them trying hardly to restrain her voice"DIFFERENT?DIFFERENT?HE GOT MY 15 YEAR OLD BROTHER ARRESTED AND KEPT IN A JAIL"She wanted to knock some sense into these people.She was too much in pain to even feel angry at them anymore.

She just sat on the bed,opposit to them looking even more wrecked then before."Why can't anyone see what is wrong with it?"Her voice slowed down with every word.it is like she is begging them to see clearly,to help her because she was lost on how to help herself.

Just when Malak extended a hand to reach her,try and make her understand,she looks up,locks her eyes with her and says,"Would you have given the same advice if Ayesha or Humaira was in my place?" and left.

The fact is that she would have if her eldest son was on the other hand and it wouldn't have been needed because Hanan and Ehan were supposed to get married.It was kind of a known secret between the elders but Ehan rebelled when he came to know about it.

They thought that he will accept it with age but he didn't.He found someone else and it was a lost cause now.

Iana's pain saddened her but Hanan's wasn't lost on her.It will be hard to console Hanan-she thought.Hanan likes him,she fell for him,hard.

IANA'S POV:

It's 8:30 a.m and I find myself entering the same place I had left so hearbroken last night.Because,I am helpless... .Dadaji had called me many times afterwards but I didn't receive his or anyone else's call.Then he left a voicemail asking me to just hear him out.Malak aunty,Ayesha and Humaira had also called.

While returning home I contacted my parent's neighbor because none was receiving calls and came to know that my home was raided by tax department and you didn't need to tell me who had done it.I still remembered his threat,"Who knows what other disaster has befallen them."

I tried everything.After returning to the dorm at that late I contacted a journalist and she got back to me right away.We talked on video call and she was interested in this.Because it was a scandal concerning a billionaire.This morning at around 5;30 while going to her office she passed away in a brutal car accident.

After a long 6 hour raid my father was arrested.I just felt numb after this.I contacted the lawyer my father had hired for my brother.Talked to him for around 40 minutes with him explaining it was a pretty bad situation.

They found a large amount of drug in his backpack,his dope test was positive and a few of his friends were ready to be witness that he sold drugs.Moreover the case would probably go on for years like most other ones.

Then asked him for advise on this tax situation and it is as bad as my brothers.

It isn't fair to ruin my brothers whole life or my father's hard earned reputation.I WILL get out of this but it isn't fair to put them on the edge of the sword for that.

I entered Dadaji's room after knocking and he seems like he was waiting for me.He seemed relieved to see me.I sat opposite him an a couch.

"Ap hame kuch kehne chahte thein,"I ask.I want this to be over as fast as I can because I don't have time.(you wanted to tell me something.)

He understands that I am in a hurry and says."This is gonna sound scary but it is the only way.Ask for 1 year till graduation.You will go away after your graduation,I will arrange everything for it."

"Run away?Leaving everything behind?"I ask incredulously.

"Bete ehi ek rasta hei."(this is the only way.)

"But how can I leave everyone."

He sighs."You have to."

"What if he finds out?"

"He won't.I will arrange for everything."

I had to leave everything.All of it.The life that I had so carefully built for myself and it was the only way.Marrying him was not even an option for me.

"Ap hame dhoka to nahi denge kiuki agar apne Diya t hum zinda nahi reh sakenge,"It is not the right choice of words because Aabroo fupi had killed herself and I see it pass through his face before he composes himself and says,"Bete,zindagi zaisi bhi ho zeene layak ha i."(Dear,however life is,it is worth living.)

"Unke sath zendegi zeene laike bhi nahi hei."In this short amont of time he has shown me hell but I wasn't aware of the much worse ones coming up.(Life isn't even worth living with him.)

"Bete,hum tumhe kabhi dhoka nehi denge.bharosa rakho."(Dear,I will never betray you.Trust me.)

He then calls him and says that I had accepted this proposal but the only thing he replied with is she knows what to do and cut the call.

BASTARD,I curs internally.He wants me to beg him...

Why don't you guys vote or comment.We writers take out hours from our schedule to write a chapter and all we ask for is a vote and a few comments if you have time.It doesn't hurt you but it motivates us.I am tired of ranting about it.My last chapter has 3 comments.

Please vote and comment.I really like knowing about your opin ion.If something is wrong tell me about it.They really motivate us to keep writing.Otherwise it is disappointing to write and get zero feedback.

Guys I am seriously tired of this.

PLEASE VOTE AND COMMENT

1.What do you think Iana will do?Will she be successful?

2.Do you think she will be able to run away?

3.Do you think Ehan would agree to this 1 year condition?

untill next time.

Astral

Chapter 13:Suffering

IANA'S POV:

"The moment I ask for time he would know something is up.He would never agree,"I can't help saying again.

He just sighs before saying,"Don't give up until you try."

"Why can't you just tell him to stop.Why can't you get him to stop?Why can't any of you help me?"i don't stop the tears from escaping me.They were tears of frustration.Pure frustration.

In the span of 48 hours or so he has made me cry more than anyone else in my whole life.I can't stand him for a few minutes.How am I gonna stand him him for a year.

"Tum samajh jaogi."That's all he says.

~~~~~~~~~~~~~~~~~~~~~~~~~~~~

After I reach their office I walk straight to the receptionists desk and ask for Ibrahim bhaijan.I don't ask for him because I have a feeling he would make me wait after all he wants me to submit.

Ibrahim bhaijan arrives within a flash.He almost seems like he pities me.I have been getting this look from this morning.Everyone in syed mansion had this same look painted over their faces and I hate it.I absolutely hate it.

"Bhaijan I wanted to meet Ehan,"My voice goes quite towards the end.

"Iana you don't have to do this."

"Do what?"

"Marry him.We will find some other way."He can't.Because if he could I wouldn't be standing here.

"Do you think I wanna do this?"My voice rougher then I intended it to be.He looks guilty and ashamed.

"Let's just do what I was here for.Can you take me to his cabin?He wouldn't receive my calls."I say to drop the topic.It's a hard one.

After reaching his cabin just before he is about to leave I call after him and say,"Bhaijan please don't look at me like this.With this pity. "These pitiful looks are really killing me.I don't wanna be their object for sympathy.

He looks hurt for a moment but then nods his head and leaves.

I wait a few moment before knocking.If I had a option I would run for the hills but I don't.

Even after hearing a come in,I can't bring myself to enter.Just the thought of seeing him makes my skin crawl.

But I have to and I do after composing myself to the best of my abilities.

He is sitting behind his desk like a king with a smug look plastered on his face which I want to knock off.

When I reach his table he motions for me to sit.

"Can we talk about this..."I motion with my hand,"proposal?"When I look up at him slightly to see his reaction,it's definitely not in my favor.

He is smiling but his eyes give away the anger.The storm that is brewing.

"You still wanna talk...."He says more to himself than me."Seems like more needs to be done."

Now he looks up and says,"I thought that I will let you off easy but you don't want that,do you?"he grits the last part.

He takes his phone dials some number and within seconds it's received when he says,"break a few bones.Torture them.Such things happen in investigation,don't they?"His eyes stay trained on me this whole time and I feel like I can't tear mine off his actions.

EHAN'S POV:

I did really let her off easy.I could have killed her whole family in a snap of fingers.But I didn't want My Hayati to go through so much trauma so I opted for less traumatic punishments. But she doesn't seem to like it.

The moment I say those words her eyes widen.Within a moment she is at my side of the desk standing right beside me.

"Please don't do this.Please just tell them to stop."

I pay no head to her actions and begin typing on my laptop.

"Are you even listening to me?JUST TELL THEM TO STOP,DAMN IT."She screams scooting to my level.

My one glare is enough to send the message.She exhales to calm herself before saying much more softly this time,"Please."

I finally turn my chair in her direction and look at her.Her eyes are red and a few tears are streaming dowm her face.Her face says how bothered she is.

"Please.."She pleads another time.

She understands that I am gonna be nonchalant until she says yes.

"I will marry you but please just tell them to stop,"she says defeatedly.

I pull her by her waist on my lap and the moment it registers,she starts resisting.Trying to get up but she can't because my hand is around her waist.I hate this.She shouldn't resist my touch.She should know better by now.

"You have a lot to lose,be careful Hayati,"I put my head on her shoulder and whisper in her ear.

She gets my warning and stops.She keeps staring at her lap like she wants to vanish.

She takes my phone from the desk and gives it to me saying,"Please stop them."

She has suffered enough for now,I decided and redial.

It's like she can finally breath after I tell them to stop.I rest my head on her shoulder and she is as stiff as a log.

I begin inhaling her.Softly nibbling her neck and she becomes even more stiff if possible.

"Please don't.We are not married yet."she chokes out.

"Do you think I care.The only reason for this marriage is I want you to have a social standing.I don't want people to label you as my mistress." I say still nibbling her neck.Her whole form trembles at my choice of words but that is the truth.

Her hijab gets in my way and just when I am about to take it off I notice her left hand scratching her right arm with so much force that they are on the verge of bleeding.I take a hold of her right hand before saying,"Don't."rather harshly.

I remove my arm from around her waist and within a moment she is off me.I take hold of her hand before she can leave and get up.Stand straight in front of her while caressing her cheek and say,"Don't ever do that again."This time in a softer manner.

She nods her head and says"I agreed to marry you.Please get them out of jail now."while still lookin down.

"And what if you change your mind?"

"I won't.I promise."She looks at me so innocently that I can't help respecting her wish.

I got manipulated by just one look of her but the thing is I want to.I want her to ask me for anything and everything she wants,seduce me with these looks and I will keep them at her feet.

"They will be free before you reach your dorm.Your driver will drop you"I say.I hired a female driver for her.

I place both my hands on her cheeks and kiss her on her forehead before finally withdrawing my hand.

She leaves as fast as she can and when she is at the door I call after her,"But be careful Hayati.The case will be there until we are married."

She just nods and leaves.

Please vote and comment.And I really appreciate every single one of you who vote and take the time to comment.

1.What will Iana do now?

2,Do you think her anger for syed family is justified?

3.What do you think of Ehan?

Untill next time

Astral

Chapter 14:Love You

I will inbox the next 500 words to the reader with most comme
nts.

I changed Aiden's name from Aiden Carter to Ebenezer Daniels.

THIRD PERSON'D POV:

The car came to a halt in front of Syed mansion.After a few minutes when she made no move to leave her driver politely informed her that they had reached home.It was only then that she looked around.It was as if she was in a trance,sitting on the far left corner of the car,almost merging with the door.

Iana looked confused at first.She couldn't understand why she was at the syed mansion.'I thought this car was supposed to take me uni.'she thought to herself.

"Why are we here?"she finally asked the driver."Take me to _____ university."

"Mam,sir has instructed me to bring you here."Her driver replied.

"Well.I am the one in the car right now,not he."She was frustrated and you could hear it as clear as day in her voice.Her driver made no effort to reply.

She just exhaled to restrain her anger,"Okay,I will go there mysel f..."Just as her hands reached the door to open it,she realized that it was locked.

At this point her eyes blazed with anger and as she looked straight at the driver,she just lowered her head and replied,"Mam I can't allow you to leave without sir's permission and he ordered that you go straight to home."

The reality of her situation suddenly hit her like a truck and her whole anger vanished in thin air leaving the smoke of despair to settle over.

It's like someone turned a switch.She just leaned back on the seat and let her hand fall from the lock.He,a total stranger to her,other than the fact that he had molested her twice within a day,was deciding whether she could attend her classes.

But the despair was relatively short lived as it left absolute panic in it's trail."Is this how my rest of the life is supposed to look like?Will I always be his little puppet?Being completely dependent on him .After every hour of hard work I put in my passion,is this how it is supposed to end?.....'her mind posed question one after another which she had no answer for and each one made her more agitated.

"no,no,no,no,not this,not to me,this cannot be happening to me ."She kept repeating to herself but it was loud enough for her driver to hear and she watched in absolute shock as Iana was losing her mind with every passing second.

She felt pity for Iana,she guessed that Iana couldn't be more than 20 and she knew what type of a person her employer or more like boss was.

And the thing that he appointed her,one of if not the best assassin and fighter in the gang to protect her and keep an eye on her,said what place she held in his life.

She quickly got out of the car to make a call to her boss because the situation with his beloved was getting increasingly worse.

"good morning,boss.Maam seems to want to attend the rest of the classes in her university.She seems really upset."She didn't say that she was not just upset,she was having a full blown breakdown."Should I take her there?"

"He thought for a few moments before saying,"Bring her home carefully after her classes.DO NOT LET HER OUT OF YOUR SIGHT."

The moment she was done with the phone call she rushed back to the car to see Iana clutching to her ears and shaking her head,as if to stop the voices.

She shaked her a few times to bring her back to reality but all she was saying was,"Leave me.Just leave me alone."

"maam he permitted you to attend college."

The moment the word permitted escaped her lips,Iana looked at her with such fierce gaze that just the intensity of those were burning her.

However Iana didn't say anything and neither did she and shortly after began driving to take her to uni.

~~~~~~

I feel the soft breeze soothing me as I rest my head on a tree with my books and everything scattered around me. At the back of uni there is a small hill. It takes a few minutes to get here but it's incredibly quite. I have hardly ever seen someone here and especially at this time in afternoon, it's 6 p.m.

Instead thinking about the recent events, I explore the mysteries of nature itself, physics. I don't wanna lose my mind again.

Abbu and Araf is out of jail now, but the case is there, as he said. I wanna be carefree for a few moments at least. I have switched off my phone and of course Zer(Short for Ebenezer) knows it.

In being fair to my family I became unfair to me. But I don't regret it. I already have thought of something and I will implement it.

Sometimes I wanna be all by myself and today is one of those. In those periods it seems too much trouble to even talk. To do anything.

Suddenly I feel a shadow on me and when I look back,i see him.

"What...?"I welp because he suddenly scoots to my level and carries me up in his arms and starts walking.

"What are you doing?"I begin panicking."Put me down. Put me down."

Within seconds he reaches his car, makes me sit on one side and sits on the other side.

"My books...."I just start when he interrupts,"they will reach you .". It was only now that I notice how angry he looks and I knew the reason welll enough.I had ditched his driver and of course switched off my phone.I had vanished but how did he find me?

He takes my right hand as I was on his right and the more I try to get it out the harder he clutches it.

"LEAVE.MY.HAND."I seethe.

He just glares at me but I keep looking back at him with equal intensity.

"It would be a shame to send them back when they just got out,"He grits.

I tear my eyes away from his and loook out the window murmuring to myself,"because that's all that you can do."

It seems to rub him the wrong way and he,very swiftly places his hand behind my head and makes me look at him,"I can do a lot more.DON'T MAKE ME."

It's after a while that I notice we are not going to syed mansion.It's a different route.

"Where are you taking me?"

Of course,he doesn't answer.

"WHERE ARE YOU TAKING ME?ANSWER ME."

I see him getting angrier by the second.He restrain his anger just enough so that he doesn't lash out right here and seethes,"You are already in enough trouble.Don't land yourself in more."

"What am I?A baby?What are you gonna do?Duscipline me?."I wanna say that but I don't.

We reach somewhere and he immediately drags me to Allah knows where.I don't even know where I am.I could hardly observe anything before he starts dragging me.

He drags me in a room and kind of dumps me on a couch before locking the door and the moment he does so everything of this morning and last night comes back.I start panicking.I don't want him touching me.Not ever again in my life.

I don't even realize that my palm starts digging in my knee before he glares at my hand.

He takes off his coat,throws it on the bed and takes a few breath to settle himself before finally sitting on the single sofa.

"I am going to set rules and you are gonna follow each one of them.

1.Obey me.

2.Never and I mean never question me.

3.Receive each one of my call.

4.Never resist my touch.

5.Don't talk to any guy other than family.

6.Don't go anywhere without informing me."

His demads are ridiculous and I automatically roll my eyes but the moment I do so,I see him standing right in front of me,bent to level and holding me jaw to look up at him.

"WHAT.DID.I.JUST.SAY?"He seethes.

I neither answer him nor take my eyes off him.

His grip on my jaw keeps tightening and it's painful.Very painful.I feel tears at the verge of my eyes but I don't let them leave.I don't let them flow.

Suddenly his look changes.Almost as if he is bewitched with me.

EHAN'S POV:

She looks bewitching.On the verge of tears yet not letting them leave,her eyes still as fierce as they could be,cheeks and the tip of her nose flushed with anger but still not backing away.Not giving up.

It's at this moment that I think,she is perfect.Perfect to be by my side and fuck,do I love her!Seeing her this strong,this resilient makes me love her more than I ever thought possible.

Of course,it meant that it will be harder to make her submit but yet that doesn't cross my mind.The only thing that does is I love this girl and I am never letting her go.Ever.

My grip from her jaw loosens and I embrace her.I scoot down in front of her and hold her as close as I can.

I kiss her cheek and just whisper in her ear,"I love you." before breaking out of the embrace and saying,"You must be hungry.Let me bring you some food." while caressing her cheek.

She seems too taken aback to say anything.Opening and closing her mouth like she wants to say something but she doesn't know what.

~~~~~~~~~~~~~~~~~~~~~~~~~~~~~~~~~~~~~~~

Out of everything that is in front of her,she just takes a sip of the orange juice before putting it down and softly saying,"I can't tell my parents about this marriage."

"What?"I almost don't hear her and what I do hear angers me.

"After everything that happened at home,I can't tell them about this,not right now."She explains.

"So...?"

Now she just looks up at me incredulous."I want them to present at their daughters wedding."

"I.DON'T.CARE."

"But I do,"She says softly while looking down.

"YOU ARE GONNA MARRY ME WITH OR WITHOUT THEM."I make sure that she hears me loud and clear.

She just softly says more to herself,"I had always hoped that my husband would respect my parents." looks up at me once,like silently saying but you are none of that and resigns to eating her food.

Knowing that I don't fit under her idea of perfect bothers me though I very well understand what she is trying to do.

IANA'S POV:

He just leaves the room leaving me to my thoughts.

I just tried to manipulate him,I think to myself.When did I become this deceptive,I ask myself.

I am not sorry that I manipulated him.He deserves far worse things.I am sad that I manipulated him.

_____

Vote and comment.

!.Where do you think he has brought her?

@.Do you think her manipulating him is okay?

#.Do you also think that Iana is becoming deceptive?

$.Does Ehan's moments of softness make you like him more or can you see past it?

%.Do any of you miss Ebenezer.(Aiden)

Untill next time,Astral.

Chapter 15:Nothing more to say?

I ANA'S POV:

It's been almost a hour and half since he left,locking me in here.I can pick locks but I am saving that for a more critical time.So,I just decided to wait for him.

But now I am seriously getting irritated.It's late and I wanna leave.

I get up from where I was sitting and knock a few times on the door,asking someone to unlock it or help me but of course no reply.

I go back and sit by the window resting my head on the windo wsill.Night is always comforting to me.This darkness is somewhat familiar.It feels like home because it is in this darkness that I have always sought comfort.

After sometime I finally hear the door unlocking.The first thing he does after entering is glare at the uneaten food.He walks up to me,grabs my forearm drags me to the table and makes me seat.Soon ,the remade food appears.

"Eat,"Is all he says while glaring at me.He had told me to finish the previous one.

"I don't want to,"That is true.I really don't wanna eat.

He just smiles hearing my words,the sickening smile that sends shiver down my spine that something bad is gonna happen,"I would love to make you eat, Hayati ,but I don't think you will love it as much as me."

That's all he needs to say to make me eat.But being the person that I am, I am more playing with it than eating it and him staring at me doesn't help.I don't like people bossing me around.

He just sighs before saying,"Eat and I will give you a good news."

Now I look at him,'Is he playing with me'I ask myself,lost in my thoughts.I don't know what I did that makes a smile break out on his face.I frown at this sudden change and he states,"Gosh,you are cute."

It makes the insides of my stomach turn,like this whole ordeal is normal.Like we are some normal couple.

After I am done eating he says,"We are gonna get married tomorr ow.."Is this supposed to be the goood news??This is beyond bad.

"What?You can't.."

"LET.ME.COMPLETE" He grits each word . It's hard to sit back and hear him talk when he is uprooting my entire world.

"You will sign the nikahnama tomorrow but the official marriage can wait until you tell your parents."

"Tomorrow? Like tomorrow? That is too fast. No,you can't do that." I keep babbling,too much in my own world to notice the change in his dememanor.

"WHAT WAS THE FUCKING PROMISE HAYATI?"His voice booms in the room,succesfully shaking me out of my thoughts.

"WHAT.WAS.THE.PROMISE?"He grits his question when I don't answer the first one.

"That I would marry you...."

"Then why are you resisting now?"Because you are the last person I would ever marry and I will do whatever I can to avoid that.

"But tomorrow is too soon.It's..tomorrow."

EHAN'S POV:

"Do you think I care about this marriage?"I mock."Do I seem religious to you?The only reason I am marrying you is so that people don't call you my whore.What,you wanna be called my whore?It doesn't matter if I get married to you or nor.You were mine the moment I saw you.I will touch you,have you either way."And that is the truth.

But I don't miss how her eyes widen at my choice of words.How her whole form shakes,how her hands fist,how she closes her eyes for a moment as if my words are a hit to her dignity.But she needs to learn.

After composing herself she softly but with clear conviction says"I hate you.I hate every bit of you,everything about you and I would never marry you in a million words if it was up to me."

I bend down,my face within inches of her,keep my hand on her cheek softly caressing it and say,"I haven't given you any reason to hate me yet,wait untill I do."

She just faces the opposite direction,out of my reach.

I bring her back to Syed mansion because she would never spend the night there and I don't trust her enough to leave her at the dorm.I doubt if she would run away considering the consequences but people take rash,foolish decision in these situations.She is gonna live here after marriage anyway.

After I am back in my room,I make a few calls so that she at least has an actual reason to hate me.She should know her line and she will.She will soon enough.

After freshing up,I relay the news to Dadaji and he just looks fed up before asking,"Where is she?"

"In her room,"is all I say.

It's late by the time we return,everyone is in their room,the atmosphere seems gloomy.

When I tell my parents I am met with a much happier mood.Both of them congratualate me and tell me that they have always loved Iana.Dad seems a bit more hesistent.he had also talked to me this morning but he knows well enough that I won't change my decision.

None mentions Hanan and she doesn't know yet.She is still in office.I have always said no to that idea and marriage with My Hayati just seals the coffin.

I work a bit more before going to sleep.

Urgent knocks at my door awake me.It's what?4 in the morning. She already knows.

I take my time freshing up before finally opening the door.

"Is My Hayati that desperate to see me,"I tease her.I am in a pretty good mood.In mood for forgiveness.

She looks like she wants to kill me.

"Why did you freeze their card,stoped every transaction knowing that tax department confiscated the money?And why is my brother's face on the front page of the newspaper,why is he on every online news?Why are they making it seem like he works with a cartel?"

"Giving you reasons"I start before phrasing it more correctly,"Starting to give you reasons to hate me."

"Stop it."She orders.

"Why should I?"

I step aside so that she enters knowing that it's gonna be long but she just takes a step back.

"okay,"I say just as I am about to close the door on her when I hear,"No,wait."

I keep waiting while holding the door open when she enters with a stiff expression.

IANA'S POV:

he places an arm on my waist,his grip gets stronger when I try to remove it, and makes me sit on the couch.Then kneels on the floor in front of me,so that he is looking up at me.keeps his hands on my knees and asks me"Ab kahye,meri jan,kya chahye aapko."His question makes me wanna laugh but of course,I don't.(Now,tell me,My love,what is it that you want.)

This would melt anybody's hear but the only thing that goes around my head is how much I hate him.How deceitful he is.I curse the hour I had met this godforsaken person.Curse the hour I had entered this omnious place.

I guess the hate I feel shows on my face because his right hand reaches out to touch my face.I flinch back.

His eyes turn darker,face contorts in something more sinister like it always does whenever I step up a line.His hand that had stopped midair reaches my face,caressing my cheek.Harsh,marking his ownership.

"breaking a lot of rules,are we?"He mockes."Well,punishment is definitely overdue."

My eyes snap to his from my lap and I am sure I look shocked because I feel shocked.

It all happens so fast that it's hard to register.He pushes me back on the couch and within momments he is on top of me kissing me while his hand violates me.I shriek but does he care?No.He doesn't.

I will stomach every other form of abuse but this is what I can't stomach.He holds my wrist above my head.drinkin away my voice.

When he finally pulls up,tears are clouding my vision but I try to blink them away and I feel disgusted at him,at me,at everything.He keeps defiling me and I can't do anything.I hold myself accountable like I always do.Because I still haven't learned to be easy to myself,to be forgiveful to myself.

When I feel things come a bit more focus I see him looking at me with a satisfied expression,smilling.

Like he doen't see my tears.Like they are invisible.

"Get off me.Leave my wrist."I can't bear being in this position one single moment but it's only after telling him that the look in his eyes make me regret.

He smirks at me before burying his face in the crook of my neck,leaving wet kisses,his free hand slips inside my shirt and rests on my stomach.I go stiff as a statue.Not daring to move a single muscle.it's now that I realise the scarf has slipped off from my head.

He stops kissing my neck and whispers mckingly in my ear,while softly kissing it."Nothing more to say,"while his hand slowly move up my stomach untill it reaches my bra and his thumb slowly caresses it's hem.I can feel him smirking.

He is provoking me.He wants me to say something so that he can go even farther.Of course,he enjoys this cat and mouse game with me.I just close my eyes and face the opposite side.This time I can't help the tears.

I feel like I want to get the ground to swallow me up.He makes me feel disgusted in my own skin.Like,if I could trade bodies,I would get the hell away from this one.

he stops playing with the hem of my bra and holds my face softly making me face him.I still keep my eyes closed.I don't wanna see him anywhere near me.

"Look at me,"he softly says and I do because I can't take anymore at this moment.I just want him off me and I don't care what that takes.

He wipes my tears,kisses my forhead,holding me so delicately as if I would break,as if he didn't just molest me.He looks me in the eye,pinning me down with his gaze,with it's intensity and says,"I own you more than you own yourself.Always remember that."His voice soft but the meaning sinister.

"It's just 4:35.I wanna sleep,"he says suddenly.

He gets off me and pulls me by my hand,making me stand.

He starts walking towards the bed,pulling me with him and that's when it crosses me.he wants me to sleep with him.

I pull my hand out of his grip and take a step back and he instantly looks back.

"NO...."I say shaking my head,my voice breathless.

He just sighs"Do we really need to do this again?"

"Don't do this to me.Don't ruin me like this."I say.

"I am not doing anything,yet Hayati .I just wanna sleep"

"What would everyone think if they see me leaving this room?"It was a awful excuse.We both know no one wakes up early.

He just shakes his head as if annoyed.He walks up to me and takes me up in his arms carrying me to the bed,ignoring my shriek and every other protest.

he puts me on the bed and before I can get off,get's in himself.

He puts his arm on my stomach literally caging me so that I can't get up.

I don't even what to say.What to say so that he wouldn't assault me yet let me go.

"I can't sleep.Please,just.."He interrupts me.

"Not another word,Hayati ."he already has his eyes closed.

"Ple............."Just as I am about to say something, his eyes fly ope n.They look fierce,angry.

"If I don't sleep then I am gonna spend this time doing something else with you and you won't like it."

This shuts me up.

I lie there,counting the minutes while he drifts off pulling me close to his chest,burying his face in the crook of my neck.

I actually feel like killing him in his sleep.

Please,vote and let me know about your thoughts in the comment section.They mean a lot to me.

!.Do you think this marriage will take place?

@.What do you think will be Hanan's take on all this?

#.How do you find Ehan's behavior?

$.Do you think Iana will actually ever forgive and love him?

Feel free to point out mistakes with the writing as well as plot.

Untill next time,

Astral

Chapter 16:Botched signature

ANA'S POV:

He is a very light sleeper.If I move even one limb his hold on me tightens.Each second seems to be dragging for forever and it makes me sick,being in his bed like this.I suppress my emotions for 2 hours unless it becomes absolutely impossible to be even around him.

The moment I try to get out of his hold,his eyes shoot open and he says,"What are you doing?"

"It's almost 7.I wanna go now."

He keeps looking at me without saying a single word.

"Please.."I request.His hands cage me again as if he didn't even hear me. He buries his face in my neck and says,"You can leave after a bit more time."I feel like every bit of my skin is crawling with insects. This is not how love is supposed to feel....

When it's past 7 and he still doesn't move an inch I finally say,"It's past 7.Please...just leave me now."

My voice trembles at the end.I feel disgusted with myself.I have never been this intimate with anyone and of course he doesn't seem happy with that.What he wants is seriously beyond me.Does he want me to behave like I love him?Respond to his touches?I can't do that even if I try.

He finally gets his hands off me and at the speed of light I am off the bed,leaving.

"I didn't give you permission to leave yet."He says sharply.How can someone be this angry in the morning.I slowly turn around.He has shifted to sitting,leaning on the headrest.

He gets off the bed and motions for me,"Come here."

I do because I just really wanna get these over with.When I reach him,he takes my hand and takes me through a door which turns out to be his closet.

He makes me stand in front of it,while he stands behind me,putting his chin on my shoulder,"Choose something for me,Hayati."

I try to step away from him but of course he wouldn't let me.His hands stay firmly on my waist.

"Choose my outfit and then you can leave."

I choose the first suit that I see infront of me.I don't even notice it's colours.

He chukcles before saying,"I am not going to office today,meri jan,after all it's my marriage today."While yet again kissing my sho ulder.slipping my dress off.

"Please don't"I try to step away once again.Why does he keep doing this.How can someone be this perverted.By now he is playing with my bra strap.It makes me wanna dig a hole in the ground and leave in it for the rest of my life.

"Do you want me to drag you to bed."My body reacts as I feel,horrified and he says noticing it,"Then don't provoke me."

I choose whatever that comes in my hand and when he finally leaves me reluctantly ,I run to my room.

The first thing I do after getting in my room is get in shower.

I let the cold water run through my skin,numbing every inch it contacts.If you have ever been in ice cold shower you would know that the moment water makes contact with your scalp,it render your brain numb,washing away every single thought.

You can't think about something even if you want.It's painfully comforting and that's what I craved now.It's too painful to think about every thing that has happened or is gonna happen.

The moment I open my eyes and it lands on the geyser I hear a voice from inside me,fanit but clear-shock yourself.

"No,"I firmly stop it from growing into anything more sinister.It's hard to fight forces outside you,but it's far more harder to battle the one inside,especially if it starts turning this insidious.

****

THIRD PERSON'D POV:

Adorned with soft colors and few light heirlooms,surrounded by her to be in laws Iana looked like an angel,but she didn't feel like one.She neither felt as free nor as pure as one.

The women around her kept a happy countenance as if it was something to be celebrated and Iana a felt a surge of hate pass through her.Why could they not see her.What had changed so much in this past 48 hours?

But she wasn't the only one who felt this way.Hanan sitting a few paces away from her felt just as much pain for exactly the opposite reasons.After all,a broken heart cuts you deep,so deep that it even hurts to breath.

Her hands kept trembling the momment the pen was placed in them.Her hand just wouldn't close in around them to the point that Ayesha had to place her hand around Iana's to make it hold on to the pen.

The pen wasn't a ordinary one.It was especially made for this,Ehan's marriage a few year prior,forever to be kept as a memory but at that time everyone had assumed that the girl in possession of this would be Hanan.

It broke Hanan to see that pen in Iana's hands.She remember the day clearly when it was designed and ordered. The brides pen more or less showed her taste.She had fawned over it when it had arrived.

When the nikahnama was kept in front of Iana,she kept botching up her sign because of her trembling hands.Each word seemed to go wrong.Malak kept a hand on her shoulder saying,"It's okay."But it was not.Not in the least bit.

At this a lone tear made it's way out,landing just on the sign,smudging the already botched sign and she scribbled away the best version of her sign she could master,Iana Islam.

The only consolation that she kept giving herself was that This isn't real.It holds no importance.She will get away the moment she can.She just has be strong untill that.

Everybody left to give the them some time and Iana hoped with all her heart that they wouldn't.She hated Ehan.He was everything that she had disliked in her life.He didn't respect her one ounce and the love that he claimed was nothing but obsession.

When Ehan entered,he was mesmerized by the angel,his angelHe had said that this marriage didn't matter but if he knew that it did. Possessing her in every sense did matter,be it legal or religious.

But her tears did anger him.But something was different now.Every other time she had seemed so strong,so stubborn.Even in her tears there was strength but now there was only vulnerability and weakness surrounding her.

Iana not even once looked up at Ehan.it was as if she ignored his existence.He strode up to her and placed his hand on her head saying,"Nikah Mubarak." but how she flinched away from his touch didn't miss him.

His voice seemed harsh.Again her tears had angered him,she thought.She hated how much he made her cry and how much she cried.But this world is something foreign to her.This manhandling,this controlling,these touches.

He sat in front of her keeping his eyes trained on her for a few momments before finally deciding to leave as his presence didn't seem to be comforting her in the least bit.Before leaving he placed a chaste kiss on her forehead,lingering a bit more than necessary before saying,"Learn to accept me."much more softly then the previous time. He could give her a little time before arranging her life the way he desired.

Explanation or rant

The reason Iana kept saying that this marriage doesn't matter in the previous chapters and this one just as well is because in actual terms it wouldn't.It's mandatory in a Islamic marriage for the bride to be willing.Accept it without any pressure.It's haram to force a bride and such marriages are considered null and void.She stays haram for her husband despite this so called "marriage".

Now why bother writing this explanation?Because I have seen so many places where it's completely butchered that if I was reading it I would think that it is halal.I have seen Fl say that he might have blackmailed me with a bomb strapped to my friend but in the end I did say yes when asked this question.NO.JUST NO.It doesn't work that way and honestly these irks me so much that I couldn't help ranting.

I think when we are on a public platform it becomes your responsibility to not spread false information and I am just doing that.

!.How did you find this chapter?

@.Will Ehan be able to rearrange her life?

#.Are you hating Ehan just as much as Iana does?

Please vote and comment.I really look forward to them.They motivates us.Tell me how you find this story in the comment section.

Untill next time,

Astral

Chapter 17:Finding Comfort

ANA'S POV:

It is dark,pitch black.I can't see my own hands.It takes me a moment to realize where am I.

I stumble through the room to get to the switch.

I remember falling asleep for forcing myself to be asleep but I don't remember doing any of this.Like switching off the light,covering myself with a blanket.I don't even remember grabbing a pillow.

It is uncomfortable. I am still in the clothes from earlier, when I signed the papers.

That's what I did. I forced myself to stop thinking after something happened. Whether it did it by taking a bath or sleeping depended on the situation. But most of the time it didn't help. I still felt just as much as in pain. The urge was lingering there just as much.

So, I decided to call Zer. Talk to him. His voice soothed me. If being honest, I don't have anyone I can call other than him, not even my family.Even when Ayesha and Humaira had been my friend they weren't definitely the ones I would have turned up to.

The thing is Zer had seen me at my most vulnerable when I hadn't wanted him to but it wasn't even up to me to stop it.As if my mind had a hand of it's own,I subconsciously caress that scar.it was faded now.I had seen to it but I felt like it was still etched there.it would always be.

It rings a few times before he finally answers it.

"Hey!" His voice heavy like he just woke up but still excited.

When did I become this inconsiderate -I ask myself. It midnight and I called him without a thought but that's the relationship we had. I could call him anytime I wanted without consideration and he could do the same. We were always there for each other.

"Gosh!!Iana! I missed you! You were so busy you didn't even have time for me." He whined.

I had lied to him. Told him that there was a function here and they wouldn't let me bail out. The memory came fresh in my mind and it made me feel disgusted, humiliated at everything. With everything. His touch still lingered on my skin and it made me wanna pull a layer off. Even if I do run away, will I ever be over this?

"Yeah...Sorry."

"Hey! What happened? Are you fine?"

Damn it. I internally cursed. He could read me like an expert. Too long of diffusing different moods. That is what it did to you to have an unstable friend. You become an expert in reading their every emotion.I hate what I had done to him.

"Absolutely.Like a freshly bloomed flower on a fresh morning."

"You hate mornings and you never liked flowers."He stated a fact.It was true.I do hate mornings and flowers.I like the serenity of night.

"It was a metaphor."I could almost feel him rolling his eyes and subconsciously a smile tugged at my lips.That is what he did to me.He could make me laugh even in a situation like this.Even when I was hating my very existence I loved his with every bit in me.

Our being so intimate definitely raised eyebrows,a lot.Most people at college think that we are in a relationship.Even Ayesha and Humaira would pass occasional comments.They refused to believe that we had nothing going on and that is the truth.We don't.I love him but just not in the way they mean.

"What were you doing?"He asks.I don't know what was I doing.

"Nothing."I reply.A part of me wants to share everything with him but there is another darker part that doesn't wanna say anything about this.I don't know which side to take but the knot keeps for ming.It keeps tightening.

"I finished reading the book.Did you?"He asks.A try at conversation and then we start talking about it.We almost discuss about it for an hour give or take.Which characters we did like and which we didn't and all sorts of nonsense.

"College is off tomorrow,isn't it?"I ask.

"Yep.Hey,what are you gonna do now?"he asks.

"What normal people do at half past 1."I say while rolling my eyes.

"Stars look awesome tonight."He sing songs.

"Hey!Are you trying to bribe me?"I exclaim while another smile makes it's way/

"Yeah."he says guiltily,"I really miss you.Ayesha and Hanan keep stealing you away from me."My throat closes at the mention of them.

"Hmm...."I hum.

"Secret meeting place?Now?"he asks.He means the mountain by that.We also have a number of others but we visit this one most often.

"Ok."It's only after I assent that I wonder how am I gonna get out of here.He definitely wouldn't let me just walk out.

"Well,ok,reach there in 30 minutes."

"Ok.Bye bye."I decide that I am gonna sneak throught he back door.

We both reach almost at the same time.

"Hey!Look at you!You have gained like 30 pounds in 2 days."He jokes.

"Don't make me smack you."I warn.He fake apologizes.

He spreads a mat before sitting on it.

It's calm here.Almost soothing and the shocking bit is in this calmness my mind doesn't wreak ahavoc either.It's as if my mind doesn't wanna whisper something and break this illusion of comfort.It wants to keep up the charade that I am safe here.

"Earth to Iana."Zer says while moving a hand in front of my face.

"Can't you just be quiet for 1 second?"I ask annoyed.

"of course I can't."

"You are like a toddler."I complain.

"I am worse than them."He says while playing with a blade of grass.

"Hey,I am sorry that I woke you up."

"No worries."He says while moving a hand like swatting a fly.As if he practically wants to push those worries aside.It makes me laugh.

"What happened?"He asks,startled.

"Nothing,"I say.We fall into another silence which I am sure he wouldn't let last more than 5 minutes.

Subconsiously my eyes fall to my hand and seeing the dried ink hits me with reality.I had managed to forget about it for some time.I am pretty sure I would have to explain this outing.He knows everything about me.I am confused why he even let me out.

"hey,look at me.What happened?"His voice laced with worry.

I am sure that I look confused because he motions to my face and when I touch it,I realized that I have started crying.

I wipe it off."Nothing,"I say while trying to smile a bit.

He doesn't believe me of course.He seems just a skeptical.

"I am always there,you know.I will always be there for you."

"You can't help me."

If he had any doubt before that something was wrong,he doesn't now.he is sure.

I don't wanna tell him.It feels humiliating to share all this.it feels like it was my fault that he did all this. It feels like people would at first ask me why it was me.What I had done.I know that he never would but still I can't help feeling that.

"Do you remember..." Yet I start telling him. Because if I have to end this friendship with him, I want him to know that I had no option and that how much he means to me.

Please vote and comment.

A light chapter after many intense ones.

Untill next time,

Astral.

Chapter 18:Feels like ownership

R amadan Mubarak.

        IANA'S POV:

I return before dawn and quietly sneak in like I never went out.Every moment in this house seems to drag on for forever.It feels suffocating to even breath here.

When one of the helpers comes to call me down for breakfast,as I am late,I refuse to go.I don't wanna see anyone's face as of now.I will be relieved when I get out of this house.

Not after 15 minutes,Malak aunty enters my room with a breakfast trolley.I can't help cursing myself for not joining breakfast.I just can't look at her the way I used to.

I can't help feeling some amount of resentment for her.Not because she is his mother but because how undividedly she supported him throughout all this.She has always been his advocate.

I truly feel like I want the earth to swallow me whole.She sits on the sofa and motions for me to do the same.I hate her but I still can't disrespect her.Suppressing every bit of hesitance I go over and sit at the opposite side.

She places the food on the table.We stay quiet for a moment before she finally breaks it.

"I know you hate me."A lump forms in my throat and with every bit in me I swallow it.It's not what she said,it's how true her words are.I do hate her.I stay quiet.

"Trust once broken never returns.You will never again trust me neither will you ever look at me the way you used to.I know that.But I still love you.You are the daughter that I never had."

"Would you have doomed your daughter to the same fate."For a moment I feel like she didn't hear me.

She sighs."It wouldn't have changed anything."meaning it would have turned out the same even if she had intervened.But she didn't and that's what matters.

"You fight for the things you love,the ones that you deem worth fighting for,though you might lose anyway."

She doesn't say anything for a excrutiatingly long moment.Then she gets up and pecks my forehead slowly saying,"You fight for their safety,sweetheart,and sometimes it lies in surrendering."

For a moment I have the urge to pull back but I don't.

The food stays untouched untill a maid comes an hour or so later to take it out.She seems hesitant when she says that I didn't even touch anything.

"Choti begum apne kuch nahi khaya?"

I close my eyes with irritation.I hate this tittle.it's like they don't wanna let me forget it.Also I know that it's gonna reach him that I didn't eat.

I sigh and say,"I will have lunch."i wanna say don't tell him but I will have to swallow my pride for that.

She just bows and leaves.At lunch I do have lunch with them.Being as invisible as I can.I don't want to see any of them and I don't want any of them to see me.I just wanna leave.When I am done and I am leaving,Ayesha tries to approach me but I just can't.Not now,maybe not ever.

At night,I am sitting on the bed cross legged.A book sprawled in front of me and I am no where near finishing it than I was when I started.Everything seems chaotic.Everything is going out of my control and I hate that.I like to have control of my life.

That when I hear a knock and I know it's him.He doesn't knock like a normal human being would,to ask permission.He does to let you know that he is entering and of course he has the keys to my room.

The moment he does I know that he is angry.He smiles at me but his eyes seem angry and somehow it looks even more scary.In a few strides he is across the room and in front of me,towering over me as I am sitting.So,last night's backlash is coming now.

His one hand reaches my my hair,while his thumb caresses my cheek and he places a kiss on my other cheek before settling himself in front of me.I have the urge to wipe it off but I also have the sense that it would lead to some consequences,I wouldn't like.

It's now that I notice he has something in his hands.He takes out a ring and softly holds my hand to put it on me and I instinctively pull it off.I shouldn't have and it wouldn't help either way,I know.

"I am sorry,"I murmer before forwarding my hand again and he says,"Good girl."That in itself makes me wanna pull my hand back again.But I just sit there indifferent.

Then he gets something else as well,a choker.

"I don't wanna wear it."I can't help saying,it has his name carved over it.It feels like his ownership.

"I wanted to but a collar with Slave or Sex toy written on it as you seem to be forgetting your place."He lets the warning hang in the air.I glare at him and if I could I would have killed him.

"I am not your slave or sex toy."

He chuckles,"Hayati,you are.You are mine to love,fuck and do whatever the hell that I want to."His eyes flash when he says that.

"Hayati,my life"I let the word hang in the air,"You definitely treat your life very fickly Mr. Syed."

"It mine to do as I please,Hayati."he puts force on the last word.

He reaches put to put the choker around my neck and I will myself to be still.He moves closer to me.So close that his breath fans my cheek to lock it in place though he didn't need to.He could have just turned it around.

When he is done,he doesn't move away.His one hand reached my shoulder and he slowly kisses my collarbone.

I as softly as I can,push him away,as to not anger him.He is here molesting me and I am gauging his mood as to not make him angry .That's what helplessness does.

His hand snakes around my face and he reaches in to kiss me but I pull back.Even with this overwhelming helplessness I can't stomach the thought of letting him touch me.Last days asaults are still raging in my mind.

"You are my wife."He says smillig but his eyes look furious.

"No,"I shake my head.Tears brimming but I don't wanna cry.

"What.?"

"No."I say more clearly,"Don't touch me."

"You don't get to decide that."He says like he is knocking sense into me.

In the span of a moment,he pushes me on my back,my hands above my head and starts his torture.I try to zone out because no matter what I do,he won't stop unless he wants to.When his hands reach under my shirt,I snap back.It's cold against my skin but I feel like it burns me.

"I like it when you are conscious,"I can feel him smirking against my skin while saying that.

When he pulls bac, he joins his forhead with mine,"It's peaceful with you beside me."But in his peace what he fails to realize is that he is burning my world down.

I feel like he is gonna leave but he doesn't.he rolls off me and lies beside me.His hand snakes around my waist and head and he makes me turn around so that I am facing him.

I am shocked.Why isn't he leaving.To my horror he closes his eyes like he is gonna sleep.

"Aren't you leaving?"

"Shh,Hayati,sleep."

"I can't sleep with you,like this."

"You are not sleeping with me,you are sleeping beside me."

"No,I am leaving."I say while trying to leave.

His hold tightens and his eyes snap open,"I really wanna fuck you,as of now but I am satisfying myself with just being beside you because I know you wouldn't be able to take it.But if you are so uncomfortable I can gladly backtrack."

I shake my head and now I tears cloud my vision because it seems like walking on a double edged sword.There is no safety.

"That's better."He says while again closing his eyes.

"Switch off the lights."I think about leaving this room altogether but he beats me to it."Don't even dare thinking about it.I will gladly drag you back and satisfy my needs."And just like that the idea eva porates.During all this what I do think is that,I would like to see the look on your face when I will run away.

Vote and comment.It's Ramadan guys, Show some kindness to your author.

!.What do you think about this chapter?

@.Iana's relationship with Ehan's Family-Any comment on that?

#.Do you think Ehan is going easy on her or too harsh on her?

$.What do you think Zer(Aiden) will do?

Untill next time,

Astral

Chapter 19:Her master,is he?

ANA'S POV:

Even though my whole body is screaming at me to fall asleep,I can't.It just won't shut off whereas he is sleeping as peacefully as you possibly can.I lie there stiff as a log untill I finally pass out.

When I wake up in the morning,it takes me a while to remember that where am I.So,my soul almost jumps out of my body when I see him lying beside me,smilling at me.Then,it takes me still more time to remember that I have college and I will probably be late.Checking the time just proves my doubt right.

Just as I am about to get out of bed,he gets a hold of my forearm and asks me,"Where are you going?"

"College."He still doesn't let me go.

"I am already late,please just let me leave,"I say motioning at my arm.

"You will not be going to college anymore,"he says nonchalantly while he gets up himself and makes his way to the sofa.

"what?"I look at him dumbfounded still trying to make sense of his words.

he spells out each word like he is talking to a child.

"Why?Like why?"I am sure I still look dumbfounded and I am trying my best not to lash out.So much for independence.I literally moved to the opposite part of the world just to be out of my family's control only to land myself in this.

"Where were you last night?Do you think that I don't know.I am letting you off far more easier than I should."He says.

"Is this because of that?If it is then it won't happen again."I takes every ounce of my willpower to say this.To beg him for something that is rightfully mine.This life is rightfully mine.The one that I have earned.

"You will not because I don't want you to.You can be home-schooled."

"Do I look like a teenager to you."I am trying to be patient but he is getting on my nerves.

"You are basically 19."he smiles like he is in reality amused.

"Whom you being a 28 year old adult married."I shoot back.

He cocks an eyebrow.He is still being playfull.does this seem funny to him.

I take a breath to calm myself."Don't take my decisions for me.You don't have the right yet."

"You will ask my permission to take your decisions before I ever ask for yours."He smirks.Knowing that he has the upper hand.

"AND WHO IN THE ABSOLUTE HELL ARE YOU TO DO THAT?YOU ARE NONE TO ME."I can't stop my voice from getting louder each second.

Within a moment he is right in front of me,his hand reacing for my face,"I am your master."He says as a matter of factly whereas there is a evil glint in his eyes.

"Don't touch me.DON'T.TOUCH.ME.FOR ONCE MAIN-TAIN A GODFORSAKEN PERSONAL SPACE WHILE TALK-ING TO ME."To get away from him,I back up against the side table knocking everything on it.I am in total hysterics now.

"Hayati,listen to me...."he says while he reaches out to touch my cheek, trying to somewhat comfort me but that is the last thing his presence or touch does and I try to back away even more while the table is still blocking my path.

He inhales trying to calm his nerves."You are not going to college and that's final.I will talk to you when I get back."He says before making his way out and locking the door from outside.

I slide down the wall.I decided to wait 1 year so that I could get my degree otherwise it would be hard to get a job but here he is destroying my whole life.Everything seems to be going out of my control and the anger bursts,bllazing,hot.I feel like it consumes me as a whole.Burns me and it will keep burning me unless I have every-thing in control.

Suddenly my eye falls on the ring that he made me wear and without thinking anything I take it off.In absolute anger I throw it away and next comes the choker.

I don't bother taking the choker off gently.I tug at it as harshly as I can and I feel it tear and bruise my skin.I throw it as well and I don't know where any of them ends up.

After what feels like forever I decide to reach for my phone.I don't know what I intend to do with it but it's only then I notice that it's not here.he has taken it.I can't help cursing under my breath.

The whole day passes like this.The maids come and go carrying my meal because I refuse to eat.I just want a break from all of this.I just want all of this to stop.

Sitting in one corner of the room I don't notice when I fall asleep.

EHAN'S POV:

The first place I head off to after going home is her room.The room is beyond hot.She didn't bother switching on the ac.It's dark here,pitch black dark and when I switch on the lights I see her sitting in a corner her knees drawn up to her chest and her head resting on her knees,her hands around them.

She seems like she is sleeping.The first thing I do is switch on the Ac.She still hasn't taken bath and;She is in the clothes from earlier and she hasn't eaten anything.

The maids that I hired for her are turning out to be useless.

I sit facing her on the floor and it's like she feels my presence and it startles her awake.When her eyes land on me,at first she looks confused and then angry.

She faces the opposite direction yet again keeping her head on her knees.She took off or more like tore off her ring and choker.I know that already but the punishment has to wait for a bit.

"How is homeschooling different from going there yourself.it will save time."

"I don't want it."she sniffles like a kid and she sounds really cute.So cute that I wanna pull her in my arms and hold her close but of course now is not the time.She is already sitting in the furthest corner of the room.

"Let's get you bathed and a dinner and then we can talk about it."We are not gonna talk about it.There is nothing to talk about here.Hearing me she glares at me.

I softly try to touch her face,"Meri jan keu itno jiddi hai ap?"I ask myself more than I ask her.(my love why are you so stubborn.)

She scoots further away.She isn't gonna take a bath by herself and neither is she gonna eat.That's clear.

I swiftly take her in my arms and carry her to the washroom,placing her in the bathtub.She looks shocked.

"Wh..what?"She stutters.

The water soaks through her clothes making everything see through.When she notices my eyes wandering around,she folds her hands on her chest.

"Leave..."And I should because any longer and I might lose control.I love her but I also desire her.I want her to be mine in every sense.Just mine.I want to posses her though I already do.

If she was normal I wouldn't have agreed to this unofficial marriage,neither would I have given her this time.I would have had her
by now.On the very first night.Actually even before that.

I wouldn't have waited this long to send the proposal.I would have
shown her what real pain looks like,maybe killing someone she loves
so she would know her boundaries.But I can't because too much
pressure and she might break.

Just as I am about to leave I see the wateraround her calf is gettng
tinted red.She cut herself.Again. EVERYONE HERE IS USELESS.

I feel like dragging her to my bed and showing her who she belongs
to.She has no right to hurt herself but I control my anger.

My hand reaches her calf and I pull the pant leg up,exposing the
cuts.My thumb glides over every one of them and now when I look
at her she looks anxious.She tries to snatch her leg away but my
hold tightens and she winches.There are already so many marks from
previous ones.

I move closer to her,my face right in front of her and ask,"Where
is it?"She knows what I am asking about.How she got her hands on
something sharp is the question.

She doesn't reply.My hold tightens.My love is getting on my nerv
es.First the ring and now this.

I reach her neck and softly start kissing her,She turns stiff.

I bite her neck.leaving my mark while again licking the wound.She
screams.I know it hurts.I want it to hurt.

"Where is it Hayati?"I say in between.

The moment my hand reaches inside her shirt,she screams,"Stop."

I look at her for her answer."It'...t's in my..y bo..o..oks."

"You have 20 minutes,come out within that time or I won't mind coming in."

She is hurt and someone needs to pay for it and they will.Her maids should consider themselves lucky if they can walk out alive.

Vote and comment.

!.How was the chapter?

@.Who do you think would cave in this situation?

#.What do you think the punishment would entail.

Guys,please give me your views on this chapter.I keep looking forward to them.

Thank you all for

your vote and comments.

Untill next time,

Astral

Chapter 20:Submissve and subservient

- -

S he doesn't get out after 20 minutes.Am I surprised?No.I expected that.She gets out after another 10 minutes and a warning.I
am sitting on the couch,dinner served before me.

when she gets out,she takes one look at me and then as if contemplating stands there still.

"Come here,"I order.

"I don't want to eat."

"Hayati,here.This instant."

"No.Go away."

I pinch the bridge of my nose.I am trying to be patient here.I
swiftly get up,making my way to her.When I reach out to take her
forearm,she takes a step back.

"No,"She shakes her head."Please,just leave me alone for one day
.Just one."she almost begs but why would she wanna be away from
her husband for even one day and why does she think that she can.

When I again reach out she almost screams,"NO.DON'T TOUCH ME."crouching down on the floor,now crying.

And that's my limit.I crouch right in front of her and take her chin in between my fingers,making her look straight at me.She still tries to scoot further away but my other arm snakes around her.

"I dare you to say,"Don't touch me." one more time and you would be spending tonight in my bed but you won't be sleeping."

That shuts her off.I take her to the couch making her sit on my lap .She opens her mouth to complain but my one glare is enough.After making her eat and go to bed,I return to my room.Tonight she will be the one coming here.I will make sure of that.

I don't eat because well,my hunger has evaporated and I am craving her but that has to wait.I haven't done nearly anything and she is already crumbling.

Soon after there is a knock on my door.Urgent.I open it to find her.She looks almost desperate.I keep the door open AND GO Back to my work.I was working on my laptop in my room.She follows my in and my one look at the door tells her to shut off the door and she does.I like her like this.submissive,subservient.

She enters and kneels on the opposite side of the table looking up at me,"Please,I will never do anything like this again.Where is he?"I ignore her.

"I am sorry.I am really sorry.I will never take off that ring or chok er.Just.."My eyes wonder over her neck which is still empty and she notices it."I-I will wear it the moment I find i-it.I just can't find it."She sounds frustrated now.Of course she can't.It's with me.

"Please,what do you want?Just tell me."I keep on ignoring her.

She keeps hyperventilating now,thinking what else to add to the list."I will never cut myself again."She wouldn't do this again either way.I won't let her.

"I will never disobey you.I-I..."

"I promise.Anything,anything just where is he."

Now she crosses the table and kneels in front of me to look right at me.She keeps the laptop aside,looking right in my eyes which she never does,"Please.."She whispers.

"Kiss me."I order and she hesitates.I just smile at her,telling her that she will still disobey me and when I reach for the laptop again,within a moment she takes my face in her hand she keeps her lips on mine. She is clueless.

My hands reach her face and I push her on the couch.My one arm supports my body and the other one snakes in her hair.She lies there motionless and let's me do whatever I want.I let go of her hair and tug at her scarf pulling it off her and my hand instantly reaches her chest.Fondling her.She almost chokes on her breath but stays still nonetheless.

"Fuck!"i can't help cursing under my breath.She is beyond perfect and she isn't wearing a bra because I didn't give her one.My other hand reaches her trousers.I am losing control.I didn't plan on having her so soon but now I don't know.I am so arounsed that it's almost painful.

I break the kiss and look up at her,panting.My one hand on her breasts and the other on the hem of her trousers.Her eyes sre focused on the ceiling.

"look at me,"I command and she does.I fingers start expertly playing with her nipples and she stiffens.Her eyes lock on mine with so much helplessness,I smirk at her.She looks alluring like this,under my mercy.I wanna tear these clothes off her and have her.It's a torture having her and yet not.

I would satisfy myself with someone else but now I can't look at anyone that isn't her.

I push myself off her because if I stay another moment then,I will lose control.She still lies there motionless.

"Fuck!I need a shower."I say to myself.

After a few moments,She sits up now,looking down at her lap.She is trembling and so are her hands.She refuses to look up anywhere from her lap.

Shit!Maybe I went too far.When I reach my hand out again to touch her,she flinches but doesn't pull back."Why does my touch bother you so much.You have no idea how much I desire you.How much I wanna ravish you yet I am giving you time.But if you keep up with this behavior I don't know how long I will be able to."She stiffens but still doesn't move a limb.

I reach for the ring and choker and put them on her again.I am confident she won't ever dare to take these off.Not after what happened and not after what is gonna happen.

"Go sleep,"I order and she gets up to leave.

"Where are you going?Sleep here."

She doesn't argue.She just goes and lies there on one side whereas I go for a bath.

IANA'S POV:

When he returns,he hugs me from behind like second skin.His skin feels cold.His arms wrap around my stomach.He softly kisses the side of my neck.His hair is still wet and I shiver at the contact.

"I want you in this room within 9 every night,no matter what.If you don't....", he let's the warning hang in the air.

He wraps his hands even tighter around me and soon he is asleep whereas I lie awake though I am tired beyond explanation.Someti mes,I just want him to be done with his torture.Just do whatever he wants so that I wouldn't have anything that I can lose.

But who am I kidding,as long as we are alive we always have something to lose,if not anything then life itself which however awfull still seems precious.

Vote and comment.I am excited to know about your thoughts in the comment section.

!.What do you think about this chapter?

@.What do you think he did or is gonna do?

Untill next time,

Astral

Chapter 21:At His Mercy

ANA'S POV:

A bit before morning,sleep engulfs me.When I wake up it seems late.But how does it matter,I don't have anywhere to go.

He is already awake and dressed.when he senses that I am awake,he makes his way up to me and kisses my forhead.I don't bother moving away or getting up.

Everything seems too much work.Getting up,moving even speaking.

He swiftly takes me in his arm and carries me.We pass through a door,to the adjoining room and he puts me down there,hugging me from behind,his chin resting on my shoulder.

"Your room.Since you would be staying here for some time,I couldn't have you so far apart."

"I-I don't want it."Of course I don't.It's connected to his room.But how his hold tightens tells me that it isn't an option.

it's painted indicolite,furnished exactly the way I want but yet I hate it.That's the nature of force.You would hate it even if you would have otherwise loved.

"Can I bring my things here."

"They already are."But no.Nothing that belonged to me is here and I look at him questioningly.

"Everything that you do need is here."That's what he is trying.Wash away the life I previously had.

"Just a few things.Maybe the frames and soft toys "I look at him sideways.

"No."

"Please,I really....."

"I said no.They were gift to you by another man and you want me to deal with that?"A few soft toys were given by Zer but nothing else yet I know that he won't let me.

I shoud feel awful,terrible about it.But I don't.This feeling,No actually, this inability to feel anything slowly starts from my fingertips untill it claims my very heart and then I stay confused whether it was better to feel that gnawing pain or nothing at all.

He ushers me in the closet.

"Take a bath and then we will have breakfast,"He says while picking out my clothes.Colour coding with his.Then he opens a drawer filled with inners and I shut it instantly,still keeping my hand over it.

"Please..."I softly whisper.It's humiliating.

He looks at me like I am crazy,"I bought these for you."

He removes my hands and picks them according to his liking.He leaves after pecking my forehead once again.

I take my time taking bath.Somehow,neither do I wanna get out nor do I wanna face him.

When I get out,the food is already served.

"Come here,Hayati,"He orders.

I do because right now,I am out of options.

He pulls me on his lap and starts feeding me but I don't resist once because I need something from him desperately.I need to know where my baby brother is.I need to know if he is fine.

"Can I have my phone?"I ask as politely as I can muster.

"Sure,"he smiles at me.He puts me down on the couch and then brings a phone which seems brand new and hands it to me.Again sitting down and pulling me closer to him,

"It's no-ot my ph-hone,"I say hesitantly.

"It is,from now on,"The numbers that you need are saved here.I feel like banging this very phone on his head but I don't.

I switch it on and the first thing I do is call home.Araf has been missing since I tore of that godforsaken choker and cut myself.

I have never heard Abbu so distressed than at that moment.He sounds tired and broken.I will never be able to forgive myself if he harms My baby.

Abbu told me that at around noon they found him in a dump.An anynomous call.He was badly beaten.His ring finger of left hand was broken because I took the ring off.His calf had cut marks exactly like

I had inflicted on myself except they were deeper and he had broken his left leg.

Abbu has sent me pics and reports and as I was looking through them,I didn't realize I was crying untill he wiped my tears.I didn't bother asking him why he did so.I know already.

"Look at me,"He says softly but at this moment I wanna strangle him with my own 2 hands but I keep my calm.

"I don't appreciate you disobeying me or talking to me the way you do.You will learn to love me,respect me and listen to me because you belong to me and as long as you do that everyone will be fine.Is that understood?"He says softly while caressing my cheeks.I am still sitting on his lap sideways.

I nod my head because that's all I can do right now.,

"Words Hayati,words."

"Yes,"I finally whisper.

"He will be fine.The best doctors are treating him,"

He pulls me to his chest making my head rest right above his heart.He keeps handling me like a rag doll and I let him.I am at his mercy but for how long?Time will tell.

Sorry for the short chapter.Eidi in advance,Now give me mine but voting and commenting a lot.

!.How was the chapter?

@.Thoughts about the characters?

#.How would you rate this story?Please,bestow me with your reviews.

This chapter is dedicated to   .I am really sorry that I couldn't upload then but it really warmed my heart to see that I have readers who are eager to read my story.I in all truthfulness,don't deem it as so.

Untill next time,

Astral.

Chapter 22:vulnerable

ANA'S POV:

I keep turning the pages unable to study.I came in his room exactly at nine but he is yet to be here.I am scared of him and disgusted by him.Just his sight is enough to make me sick.

That's when he walk in and locks the door.A satisfied smile crosses his features when he sees me seated on the couch.

He discards his blazer while walking up to me and takes a sit right in front of me.

"Good girl,"He praises while his fingers entangle themselves in my hair and his thumb caresses my cheek.

I gave up wearing a scarf on my head because he tears all of them and he has warned me not so gently.Now one is just wrapped around my neck.

I keep my eyes trained on my lap.He takes my chin between his thumb and forefinger and makes me look at him.

But I always had a eye contact problem.I can't hold anyone's gaze let alone his.So,I resort to looking between his eyebrows.

"Not my eyebrows Hayati,my eyes,"he chuckles.

I am sure I look distressed because I do feel distressed.I can't do that.I have never been able to.

I don't know what overcomes him but suddenly he embracess me so gently as if I would break and inhales me,his face in the crook of my neck.This times are when I hate him more.When he behaves like we are normal.Like he is normal.

it makes me self conscious.This close proximity.I really wish he wouldn't do this.I can't bear his touch whereas he seems to love mine.

"Let's go take a bath."He says.I almost shriek and pull away at this."I-I h-ha-av-ve ta-ake-e-en a bat-th,"I stutter.

He laughs at my flushed state.Genuinly laughs.Not a chucle or mock."But as far as I know,you love midnight baths.Even at around 2 or 3."Stalker!Is there anything he doesn't know?

"I know everything,"he says mischieviously as if reading my mind .He gets dangerously close to my ear and whispers,"I even know the exact dates of your period."

My eyes widen at this.But before I can react He gets up and walks to the washroom abandoning me to my thoughts for torture.

After I don't know after how long he comes out but to horror in nothing but a towel wrapped around his torso.My eyes widen at his state and I avert my eyes instantly.I have never seen a man in this condition.

I keep my eyes on my lap wheres my cheeks become heated..Why did he do that.The closet is attached to his washroom.He laughs at my flushed face.

"My sweetheart is too innocent,"He teases.He walks up to me and drags me to his closet,"Choose something for me."while hugging me from behind.

He is naked and his body is ice cold.His face is already in the crook of my neck and I take a step forward to get away from him but his hold tightens.

"We don't need to repeat yesterdays lessons,do we Hayati?"his tone sounds menancing and I shake my head instantly,tears clouding my vision just remembering it.

"Then behave like a good little wife,hmm?"

I stand rooted when he nudges me a bit,"Choose.......though I don't mind standing like this the whole day."

I don't really notice what I choose and hand to him so that he would let me leave.And when he does I almost run inside.

After that we have have dinner which he feeds me or forces me to eat.Then sleep,but it doesn't come to free me from this cruel world.

My eyes stay rooted to the ceiling like every other night.This has become my constant companion.It has been a few weeks since.I just can't sleep anymore.Being so vulnerable beside someone so wicked scares me.My body just won't shut off

Sometimes,when I am lying next to him,this sudden disgust would overpower me like I wanna get out of his hold and peel a layer of skin just to get his touch off me.I always force that bile down my throat.

Other times,I would suddenly be despaired to an unimaginable extent by remembering what he did and what he is gonna do.Tears would flow freely.While I burn in my own misery,he would most times be lost in his paradise.

There would also be times,he would wake up.He is a very light sleeper so I have to be extremely quite. when he does,he would just make it worse.He would hold me so tightly that it would leave bruise saying things like how he owns me and everything and how the soon-er I get used to him the better or there would be other times,when he gets angry that I am still not used to my 'Husband's touch' or why wa I crying when he didn't even do anything yet.

In my trance I don't realize when he enters.It startles me when I notice him standing beside the bed.He reaches down to place a forhead kiss and strokes my hair while sitting next to me.

"Still can't sleep?"He sighs.He is late today,it's almost 1.

I don't say anything,he knows the answer.

Then he calls in a maid and she comes in to place a tray on the bedside table.These are the maids hired by him,who takes care of me in his language and keeps a eye on my every move in mine.

It looks like tea of some kind.

I look at him questioningly.He places a hand behind my head and another on my back so that I sit up and places a pillow behind my head.Like you would for a sick person but the only difference is that I am perfectly fine.

He brings the tea to my lips but I pull away.I really don't trust him anything.

"What is this?"I finally ask.

"It will help you sleep.It's herbal tea."But it smeels different.This house has a variety of herbal teas and none of them smell like this.

"No.I don't want it."I shake my head.

"You can't keep staying awake like this.You need sleep."

"No,"I shake my head.Tears cloud my vision.He sees what he is doing to me yet he keeps doing it.All the frustration come flooding back.It's torturous not being able to sleep.Being denied the only comfort you can have.

"I don't wanna be medicated."I state.

"Ruhi,It's just to help you sleep."(ruhi means my soul)

"NO,"It comes out more defiant than I expected.

This time when he brings the cup to my mouth,I shove it away so hard that it falls to the floor.

He pinches the bridge of his nose trying to calm himself down.

"I am gonna call for another cup and you are gonna drink that one."

"NO."

Now he glares at me and I match his glare.He is angry.His body language stiff.

"If you care so much about me then let me sleep by my own.Stop forcing me to sleep with you.Stop sneaking in bed with me,"Tears flow freely now.

"I didn't wanna do this but you aren't leaving me with much of an option." He says making his way to one of the drawer. When he makes his way back, I finally see what is in his hand, he is gonna inject me with that medicine.

I try to thrash around get out of his hold but he overpowers me easily and just as swiftly the siringe pierces my skin.

After that everything is hazy.

****

I slowly walk out of unconsciousness. It takes a few minutes to see clearly and another few to remember everything. The room is still dark but it's probably late.

He is sitting beside me, his back againt the headrest typing away on his laptop.

when he sees that I am awake, He keeps it beside him and turns his attention to me, stroking my face.

"You medicated me," I say to myself but loud enough for him to hear.

"It's for your own good Hayati." What I wanna do is scream and break everything but I realize I am crying when he wipes it from my face. I feel helpless but I don't like feeling helpless.

He makes me sit up and pulls me on his lap sideways, my head resting on his chest and his one arm encloses around me whereas his other arm strokes my hair.

"No leave me," I try to push him away but he when he doesn't budge even a bit. I start sobbing in his chest. clutching his collars.

"I hate you," I whisper and I do. More than anyone I have ever hated.

Vote and comment.What are your thoughts about each character?Tell me in the comment section.I would love to know.

Untill next time,

Astral.

HELP

I really don't know what to write guys.help me.I am trying to come with a chapter for so long but nothing is making sense.The ideas that I have can hardly be called fragments.

Chapter 23:Replaceable

- -

ANA'S POV:

The first night I was shocked,the second and third I threw a tantrum,the fourth I pleaded,the fifth I begged and the sixth I relented because he was not going to.I was getting tired of the injections.

He would rather medicate me then let me be on my own so that I can really sleep.No just slip into a mindless haze.That is how much he loves me.

This morning comes like any other.I slowly slip out of that haze and the first thing I subconsciousoly do is take in my appearance.I can never trust him.He chuckles at my effort.the rest of the days he would just observe me with curious eyes but today he somehow finds it amusing.

He leans in dangerously close to me, looking right in my eyes,he says,"I wouldn't do something to you while you are so out of reality because I want you to feel every touch when I do."What I really wanna do is smack the smirk off his face but instead swiftly get out from under him and freshen up.

After I get out I see him sitting with breakfast spread before him.I don't argue with him and just start eating to get this over with.Arg uing really doesn't help.

He quite literally controls every aspect of my life.From what I eat to what I wear,to who I call.I am still using that phone and it doesn't have any social media.Everything in my room though it can hardly be called that because nothing here reflects me,was chosen by him.

"Kya soch rahi hai,"He casually asks.It's only then that I realize I had zoned out.(What are you thinkinh?)

"not-th-hing re-al-lly,"why do i stammer when I speak to him?

So lost in my thoughts,I don't notice him reach his hand out to touch me.Softly caressing my cheek.I flinch because it takes me by surprise but I don't pull back.I know better than that.He would make me swallow my words and regret my actions if I did so.

Yet I can't help this disgust that crawls my skin everytime.Just being in the same room with him somehow makes reminds me that i am not pure anymore.After a few momments I slightly pull my face back hoping with all my heart that he wouldn't have those sudden changes and he doesn't.

Instead he gauges my every move while I eat.I don't know whether he takes his breakfast before me or what,but most days this is it.he would drink coffee while just staring at me and that makes me fumble even more.

Or just worse yet,feed me like I am a baby making me sit on his lap and that feels humiliating.I want the earth to swallow me whole the momments he does this.And then comes the not so offhand remarks/warnings withnessing my hesitation.

I finish it fast because he wouldn't leave unless i do.he puts his coffee mug down at the same time that i finish.His hand reaches my cheek and he places a kiss on my forhead.This has become a ritual.

"Wouldn't you kiss your husband goodbye,hayati,"seems like he intends to add something to the already existing ritual.It takes me by surprise and I look at him distressed but he is serious.Dead serious.I peck his cheek.

He doesn't look satisfied but let's it go."we will work on that."

"be good,"he adds before getting up to leave.The last part of his sentence remaind unsaid which is,"i don't like mark on my things." something that he doesn't often forget to add.

He astonishes me.One mommeny i am his queen and the other I am not any different than the furnitures he keeps in his house.One moment I am his better half,his soul,his life and the other I am his whore,his slave.So,which really is it?

I know the answer well enough yet I can't help asking.I am what-ever that fits his narrative best.

I shake this thoughts off my head and head to dadaji's room.There I give him medicine,nothing serious just vitamins and everything.i would do this when I used to visit earlier but now that I live here I do this daily.

I don't talk to anyone else in this house.They have tried to,they still do but I just can't look at them with the absolute trust that I used to.It's ruined and it will never be fixed again.

It's what you would describe as pin drop silence and the only chaos that seemed to exist is the one wrenching my heart apart.The sky is so bright,so luminous yet enjoying it seems like something faraway,out of reach because the one with whom I had enjoyed it most often has left me like I never existed.

But he was supposed to be there,the one person whom i would have bet on.

He didn't try to reach me once after that night.Not even once.I know my cell isn't with me but he knows where I am.Yet it seems as if I have faded into his past just like everyone else's.

All these days I would tell myself that he was wanna contact me.I refused to even think about it but when I came near this window today,all that burned in tears of betrayal.I finally accepted what I should have long ago.He has abandoned me.

"it's better if he doesn't contact you.That is one less person he can hurt,"My rational voice tries to argue yet my heart refuses to accept it.It's selfish but I can't help being so.He left me in a heartbeat.Even when I had met him that night and told him everything I never thought this would happen.he had promised me tha he would get me out of this.

He was supposed to walk through hell with me yet he abandoned me before the entrance itself,on the very earth.No matter what you might think,we are replaceable.All of us are.

Hi,guys.Extremely sorry for disappearing.Forgive me.I am also sorry for this short chapter but i promise to update if you guys bestow me with 30 votes and 20 comments.

Did you guys like this chapter?

!.Why do you think Zer has disappeared from her life?

@.What do you think the next chapter would entail?

Untill next time,

Astral.

Chapter 24:Master of my own heart

I ANA'S POV:

Detached from my reality,I don't notice him entering his room,but can you really blame me,he moves like a predator does through it's territory.Silent,determined.

When I feel his presence on the bay window seat before me,it snaps me out of this memeory lane or more like misery lane to throw me down another.

I am not shocked.One of his minions must have informed him."c hoti begum ro rahi hain/mistress seemed upset," and on and on this goes.I don't eat enough and he is informed.I enter the kitchen and he is informed.I don't wear the outfit he chooses and he is informed.I step out of this house even to the garden and he is informed.I step out of the line even a milimeter and he is informed.even when he isn't here he is always watching me.

He kisses me on my forhead before wiping my tear with the pad of his thumb.I hold the urge to wipe his kiss off.

"Kya hua meri jan.Kyu ro rahi hain aap?"His question makes my anger double.I feel like smashing his head on the nearby wall but I am trying so hard not to snap.

I try to get up and just walk away from him but the minute I do,he pulls me back by holding my left hand.He pulls me in his lap,his front pressed against my back.

"You don't get to walk away from me,Ever."His voice sends a shiver down my spine but I am way too angry to care.These are the moments when it's impossible to control myself.I know very well,that screaming or anything else wouldn't matter and yet I can't help.The anger,the loss of control is so overwhelming.

"leave me,"

I try to get off but he turns me around,my both hands against my back.I am facing him now.

"Did you forget who you are speaking to?"He mocks.He hands starts creeping in my dress,travelling my spine upwards.Tears brim my vision and yet I refuse to give up.

"Don't touch me,"I seethe.

"And you get to dictate that,"He cocks an eyebrow at me,still smirking.I am so worked up but that is somehow funny to him and that makes me so much more angry.

"You are pathetic."I hurl any insult I can just to hurt him.He is still smillng but now it's menancing.

"Careful ruhi,Araf isn't healed yet."

"You really are pathetic.You keep running back to the one thing that you can do.Do you ever look at yourself in the mirror?You can't get someone to marry you willingly despite so much wealth.How awful of a person do you really need to be for that to happen."

He laughed like it was something actually funny."Hayati,this marriage does far more for you than it does for me.This way you are being callled my wife but vice verse you would be called my whore and either way,it is my bed that you are gonna warm."

I felt his words peirce right through my heart.He never let's go of this chance to let me know that he would have me as his whore just a easily and by marrying me he did me a favor.

"I might become your bed warmer but I will never become your lover."It send a pang through my heart to call myself that but I have lost a lot since I have met him ,shame only being one of the very first.

The one person who was supposed to protect my modesty stripped me off it.

"You will become what ever I want you to be."he challenged.

My gaze met his for the first time on their own,taking his first name without being coerced by any fear or threat "No,Ehan.I will not."

"You might pull the strings of my destiny for now but I will always be the one ordering around my heart.It will never fall for you.You are evrything that I never wanted."

EHAN'S POV:

"You might pull the strings of my destiny for now but I will always be the one ordering around my heart.It will never fall for you.You are evrything that I never wanted."Not a trace of anger in her voice and it's calmness freezing.The first time she has taken my name but only to declare something that burns my skin.

She would never love me.I know that but yet hearing it this clearly from her own voice made me wanna rewrite her whole existence.I push her off me,leaving the room and head to my penthouse because I might do something that I would regret.

I head to the basement to pent out some of the anger.There is always someone to torture and even after being done it doesn't give me any satisfaction.

I head off to make myself a drink.I keep drinking and yet her words keep ringing.

I will rewrite this memory.She will swallow her words and she will say what I wanna hear.I will rewrite every part of her that I don't like.

With this in mind,I reach home.When I enter the room and see her sleeping,my whole determination wavers .I stumble across the room to her side and kneel beside her.There are dried tear marks on her face.My hands trace those marks on their own.

You have to be careful with her.You cannot take rash decisions-my mind warns.Once this thought occupies my mind,it doesn't seem to leave.I trace from her shoulder,to her hips to her feet.I wanna check if any new marks have showed up.

I pull her pant leg up a bit.There aren't any new marks but yet the sight is devastating on it's own.There are already so many old marks.Her calf is scarred.There isn't any space left.

I pull the pant leg down gently before doing the same with the other one and the same sight welcomes me.

"What am I gonna do with you,"I whisper to the silent room.

I take a seat across from her on the sofa.Hours pass in a trace,watching her like this.Her chest rising and falling in steady breathing.A new day arrives and passes along.she will be ecstatic when she hears about this.She has been desperate to be away from me.

When she finally opens her eyes a bit,my presence right in front of her on the couch startles her.She sits up hurriedly.She takes a few breath to calm herslef down before setting against the bedrest.

I make up my way to her,settling myself in front of her.

"Good morning,"I kiss her forhead.

"Go-o-od morn-ni-ing ,"She replies back but I see her taking in my whole appearence for a short living moment before her eyes ettle back on her lap.I know Ilook dishevled,My eyes arr probably bloodshot.

She seems nervous under my gaze.

"I am leaving for a few months,I am leaving you alone for a few months,"I correct myslef.Her eyes snap to mine.She looks shocked .The hope in her eyes,this desperation for me to leave almost makes me wanna backtrack.But I don't.

This is the last chance I am gonna give her and if she fails to accept me after this one,I won't hold myself back anymore.

I caress her cheek and she is so surprised she doesn't even pull back.

"But,"Her expression almost changes to agony,like this very word is painful,"When I come back,you will be mine in every sense without questioning anything and if you do,I won't be so patient."

"And don't ever think about marking your skin again.Eat prope rly.Stay away from other man.You won't hear from me during this time,but I will hear everything about you."I inhale her scent for what is gonna be a pretty long time and kiss her on her forhead before leaving.

Vote and comment please.

!.What are your thoughts about the chapter?

@.Do you think that he is really leaving?

#.What are Iana's day's gonna look like after this change?

Untill next time,

Astral.

CHAPTER 25:What happened?

It has been really long since I updated so a bit of last chapter.I am really sorry.I have no excuses and I am extremely grateful for all your kind words in the previous segment.I would like to request something though.Please let me know about your thoughts.If not anything then just if you liked it or not.The previous chapter got 2 comments.I was so scared that you guys were not liking it.My mind kept telling me that I took a turn I should not have and all of you hate it.After that it took me one month and all your kind words to just start writing a chapter again because I felt like you all wouldn't read it either way and you hate it.I do understand that it can be frustrating for chapters to be update that long apart.

But if you guys vote and comment enough then I promise I would be more regular.

"I am leaving for a few months,I am leaving you alone for a few months,"I correct myslef.Her eyes snap to mine.She looks shocked .The hope in her eyes,this desperation for me to leave almost makes me wanna backtrack.But I don't.

This is the last chance I am gonna give her and if she fails to accept me after this one,I won't hold myself back anymore.

I caress her cheek and she is so surprised she doesn't even pull back.

"But,"Her expression almost changes to agony,like this very word is painful,"When I come back,you will be mine in every sense without questioning anything and if you do,I won't be so patient."

"And don't ever think about marking your skin again.Eat prope rly.Stay away from other man.You won't hear from me during this time,but I will hear everything about you."I inhale her scent for what is gonna be a pretty long time and kiss her on her forhead before leaving.

IANA'S POV

I didn't let myself think.Thinking is dangerous and hoping even more so.I feel like he is playing with me.My eyes followed his back like a hawk as he vanished from my sight .I can't even get myself to blink because I feel like the moment I do,this fairytale would shatter,shattering me so much more with it.

It escaped my senses that I was crying untill a tear drop landed on the back of my hand.Is he really gone?Is he really leaving me alone now?I forced myself to not believe this because there is just a good enough chance that he doing all this just to test me.

I fall back on the bed.I feel so overwhelmed.So exhausted.But that is how I always felt these days.Too tired to do anything.The thing is I am obsessed with cleaning things,So even if I do nothing I will clean my room but now I don't even have the energy to do that.I would lie in mess for as long as he would let me,which isn't that long in case you are wondering.

I sat up and dashed for my room because I don't wanna spend another moment more in here than I have to.even this bed smells like him.Everything does.In my room I just collapse statring into space.If this is a dream I would like to live in it forever.

Not long passes before his minions enter with my breakfast.I fell like banging my head on the wall.To be truthful,hating them seems almost childish because they are not the one pulling the cords but most of the time it is the messenger who has to take the brunt of the message.because when in pain logic seems useless and mind worthless.

"Mistress,your breakfast."His minions replied.

"I don't wanna eat.Just let me sleep and take all this away."And of course she didn't find it necessary to respond to my request in any way.This is what his minions did or he taught them to do.They wouldn't argue with me or say anything for that matter.They would just stand there like a statue.

"You know what,forget it."i mumble to myself walking to the washroom.I take a bath before making my way to the breakfast.There are always too many items and of course these are selected by him.

I sawllow evrything that I can before standing up and cluelessly walking up to the bed again collaping but I can't really sleep so I lie wide awake.Almost the whole say passes like this with the meals in between.

At night After am given the sleep meidcation and it finally lures me into oblivion.When I wake up again,it is still dark.Its 2 A.M.This has been happening as the medication is starting to wear off.When he is here,I never moved a muscle because if he knew he would just increase the dose.

But today that he isn't I make my way to the window.They look just as beautiful as they always did and they are just as comforting.It reminds me of Zer and the so familiar,void in heart pain,starts.The type that has you reaching for breath.It's so painful.

And even that pain seems somehow comforting.Even when he is not with me he still soothes me.I wonder what he is doing.If he ever remembers me.I wish that he had at least once confronted me,told me that I am too broken to be around and i would have gladly let him walk off.Burt he disappeared altogether and that betrayal hurts.Turns out I didn't need to reach hell to test his friendship,earth turned out to be more then enough.

I see the stars making their their journey from horizon,to over-head,to out of sight leaving an empty sky sun.I watch every bit of it like zI am hypnotized.

I am sitting in the space beneath the staircase as an attempt to es-cape his minions.They wouldn't for the love of god leave me alone.He really is gone.It has been 3 days.Apparently he has called others to let them know.

Lost in thoughts,I don't notice Ayesha sneaking in beside me and when she lightly touches my shoulder whispering,"what are you doing here?".I jump.

"Sorry.I didn't mean to scare you....."She trails off.The silence that ensues is awkward.Really awkward.I don't know after how long we are sitting together like this and I can't just go away because I despise those maids he hired for me.

"shh.It's cold."she shivers.It really is.Very cold.

"you must be enjoying that.You love cold."She keeps running her one way conversation.

"Do you remember.........."she starts when I softly touch her hand shushing her.

"Don't Ayesha.You don't need to."

She shakes her head.suddenly tears clouding her vision."I do and moreover I want to.I miss you,"her voice breaks."We all miss you but you ignore us like a plague."

Seeing her cry makes me wanna cry as well.I miss them too.He took everyone away from me.He separated my friends from me.I was never close to my family to begin with.My mentors aren't there anymore and the ones chosen by him very carefully maintain their distance.

"Ayesha.."i begin when she cuts me off again.

"Do you remember that trip .You,me and Humaira had so much fun and none knew and sneaking in itself was the excitement.We kept acting goofy for days."

"And all the other ones that followed."I complete.

One night while I was here.Ayesha,Humaira and me all were in the game room.At first the paln was to do something fun but when the time came we couldn't really find something "fun."Slowly but steadily the conversation went downward like how we are wasting our life and within a bit of walking in our "netflix and chill attitude" was nowhere to be found Instead we seemed like depressed goofballs.

We were still scrolling through netflix.Humaira says,"see see,Here these people take these random raod trips.why don't we ever do anything like that?"She says pointing to the movie"Dumb and Dumber."

"Well,up untill now we didn't?"Ayesha prompted with a mischievous look in her eyes."Their road trip was a hell though."i say gesturing to the movie.

"Come on,Iana.Stop being negative."Humaira threw a pillow RIGHT AT MY FACE in her words to swwat the negativity away.off we went just about as we were.It was so random.It was the first time we sneaked out but definitely not the last and none till now knows anything about it.

It kind of become a ritual after that and the funny thing is none still knows.We are crazy and it was crazy.

None of us had ever thought that something like this would happen.

"How did we come here Iana?What happened?"I felt more like she was asking herself.

I wiped my tears because what happened exactly flashed my ey es."My friends betrayed me when they should have been there for me.That is what happened."

I left the corner of the staircase.It feels suffocating now.I will any- way be leaving everything behind in a few days and I don't plan on patching these bonds just so that I can be hurt once again even more.

Chapter 26:Stupid,stupid me

IANA'S POV:

I stare at my reflection.My facial indication is a clear give away that I am not pleased with what I see.I take a strand of my hair with so much disdain that if the girl on the opposite side of mirror could flinch,she would.But she is doomed to mirror my every movement.

My hair is so long now.It wasn't at all this long before.It was very short.hardly to my shoulders.But then suddenly my hairdresser refused to cut my hair.One day she would be busy so the other she wouldn't have the required products and as a hijabi it was hard to find hairdresser and then he came along.

He made sure that I didn't ever even think about cutting it.He is obsessed with my hair.I stopped looking in the mirror because everytime I would see someone I hate.It is not as much as i hate long hair as I hate the one it reminds me of.He changed everything of mine according to his wish.I didn't even dress the way I liked.It was all him.

When i was at home,I wanted to cut it but my family made sure that I didn't.they were almost aggressive about it.So,the moment I left it i cut it out of spite to be free from their bonds more than anything else.That is the thing.At home,they controlled everything that I did.Everything.

So,I ran.As far away as I could.In the end it turns out I ran a full circle.

Ayesha's voice outside my room along with her knocking shakes me out of it.Ayesha and Humaira have been kind of trying to rebuild I guess.I am not straight up rude to them but I try to avoid these.

But I guess they came at a reasonable time.

I swing the door open and before they can even open their mouth,blurt out,"Do you guys have scissors?"

"What?"Humaira asks confused.

"Scisssors,Do you guys have any?"I don't.There isn't anything sharp in these 2 rooms.Not even anything made of glass and even if there is,it doesn't break.The kitchen is always under lock now.When I had first been introduced nothing had been like this.He changed these.I wonder if they know.

But Ayesha and Humaira's confused expression tells me that they don't.There isn't a hint of worry or dread.

"Yes?"Ayeshha replies after a minute,still confused.

"please bring it.I request."

Humaira goes to bring it whereas Ayesha enters with me, asking,"what would you do wth it?"

"You will see,"I say softly because i have a feeling they wouldn't let me if they knew.

After Humaira bring it I stand in front of the mirror and before they can react cut it in one swift motion.Shorter than my shoulders.

"Iana!"Humaira shrieks.

"What are hairdressers for?!"Ayesha exclaims.

I just smile.Are they oblivious or do they just ignore what a monster their brother is.

"My hairdresser won't cut my ahir."I answer Ayesha's question.

"How dare she?!And we could have found someone else if she won"t"

"none would."

"why?"Now Humaira speaks.Seriously confused.

I can't help the look that I throw their way and that is when it clicks in their mind.Ayehsa visible gulps and Humaira looks distrought.It is only after I see their expression that it crosses my mind that I probably got them in trouble.

Like you aren't in any,my mind scoffs and truly if they are in trouble then I am in for hell.

But they didn't do anything.I think.

And you did...?My inner voice asks.

I feel someone standing next to me and it snaps me out of my la la land.

It's Ayesha.She looks like if she could she would glue every single hair back.Her expression makes me laugh though I should be really worried.

It's when Ayesha takes my hair from my hand that a memory returns.So vividly that I feel like I am living it again.

So,in one of our girls night we were bored.So unlike normal human beings who probably watch a movie or something as a source of entetainment,what did we 3 do?We cut each others hair.Did a few hours research on youtube about every single cut that exists and then applied them on each others.Turns out it takes more than a few hour courses from you tube to be a good hairdresser.

It went something lke this,when I was cutting Humairs's hair and Ayesha was reading the instructions out loud from the video,I had already seen it once,while talking to us Ayesha missed a step,and we were so engrossed we hardly noticed.it came out erratic and uneven and the same goes for rest of us.After cutting we looked like jokers and we couldn't stop laughing about it.

At was in the morning that it actually hit us what a blunder we have caused.Our hair would be ugly for weeks because we were bored.Not to mention the scoldings.

Hanan api had been livid.The thing is the elders hardly disciplined Ayesha and humaira and now me.It was always Hanan api.That is what I liked about the.They treated me as their own.they didn't shy away from marking me as their daughter.

A smile graces my lips.Even in between so much chaos I was still happy.Even in my darkest times,when my mind had been most hostile,I had been free.I shake my head before I get too lost in that memory lane.

I softly say thank you to Ayesha before leaving,my own room that is.I don't know what else to say ,so I depart to the libfrary,witha scarf on my head.That is the thing though,I escape to libray when they come to my room and vice verse.I feel sad though for doing this.

I haven't see Hanan api from the night we got married.She hates me.I know that.she has every right to.She doesn't even stay in this house.She is in one of her apartments or somewhere else.

The night before the marriage I had seen her quite literally beg him.He didn't even show an ounce of sympathy to her.The only thing he said was,Hanan don't embaress yourself anymore than you already have.

It isn't untill after Ayesha and Humaira leave that they bring my dinner.This is the way I tell time now.They are always so swift.zI feel like a puppet whose every move he controls.

But when all of his maids are entering they stop dead in their tracks,seeing me.Their expression tells me,how bad it truly is.They are expressionless,always.No matter what I did,they wouldn't react and that included thrashing this very single room twice while he was here.But the fact they these emotionless status showed any expression installs fear in me.

Their reaction is short lived,because then they proceed like nothing happnened and here tears are on their way.

I play with my food for a moment.

"please don't tell him,"I swallow a lump whispering softly.

Their usual,they don't reply.

I eat whatever I can as fast as I can just do that they would leave.

Stupid stupid me.He had given me a few months and I had to ruin that just because of hair.Now he would be back.

I spend the rest of the night in my bed crying.

A few days has passed like that and he hasn't returned so I am a bit calmer.I am staring at the sky from his library,a book set in front of me.I love nature but he doesn't like my love for nature.

"here she is,"i hear Irfan saying and i turn just in time to see Irfan entering with Ayesha.Humaira and Arham following behind.

I didn't speak with Irfan,Arhan or Ibrahim bhaijan not because I am angry with them but because he is a person who is jealous of his own brothers.

I know that Ibrahim bhaijan had tried to stop him when he first came with that proposal but beaten face and black eye was a clear indication of what went down.

Everyone anyway treats Irfan and Arhan like kids.Being the youngest in my family,I know how that is.

"Let's go out,"Arhan is the first to say.I don't know what to say.Wo uldn't it be awkward.It has been months and we are still on no easier terms.

But the truth is,I am desperate to get away from this house.In which everything reminds me of him and his minions who keep a keen eye on me.But I can't they wouldn't let me.

"I can't.If I go they would accompany me and it would ruin your trip."Let me explain to you the way I go anywhere now,be that gard en.If I am going by car,then there is that female driver who is always there and a female guard on he passenger seat and another one beside me.Then ther would be a car behind me with male guards and the door and windows are always locked.If I even wanna roll it dowm I have to request them.They get out open the door for me and then I get out and wherever walk there are 2 guards around me and I behind me.

"Who wouldn't,"Humaira asks confused.

I explain the same to them.

"Kiske itni himmat hai jo tumhe roke,".It makes me laugh not because it's funny but because of the irony.

"Hum dadaji se puchenge,"Humaira storms off while Irfan sits across me.

"kya parrahi hoo?'

"I was rereading to kill a mockingbird."I tell him the same we make small talk with hi, untill Humaira returns and she announces,"Dadaji ne kaha hai ki tum ja sakti ho aur tumhe koi nahi rok sakta."She glares at the maid behind me.I smile,waiting to see this unfold as this would definitely not be the end.

"Mam,I don't think mistress can.We have strict orders."I lean back a little.

"Now it's Ayehsa's turn to rage,"The brothers are quite.He is easier with his siters then his brothers.Especially Humaura and Ayesha,2 younest girls.But when was is outrage when he isolates me from everything,even them.When he molests me every night.Then they vanish in thin air and now that he isn't here this outrage on the messenger rather than the dictator seems hypocritical.

Unable to make Ayesha understand the maid just softly syas,"Mam,you do realize that if something happens to mistress then we wouldn't be the only one facing the consequences." now Ayesha stopa.colour fades from her face.By if something happens to ger she means more if she runs away then unwanted dangers.

Ayesha looks at me,trying yto gauge my intentions and i can't help the ghost of a smile that overtakes my features.This truly is entertainment.